I0547504

THE GENERAL'S AMBITION

MARCIA LYNN McCLURE

The General's Ambition Copyright © 1993, 2010, 2017
by Marcia Lynn McClure
www.marcialynnmcclure.com

All rights reserved.
All rights reserved. Except as permitted under the US Copyright
Act of 1976, the contents of this book may not be reproduced,
transmitted, or distributed in any part or by any means without
the prior written consent of the author and/or publisher.

Published by Distractions Ink
1290 Mirador Loop N.E.
Rio Rancho, NM 87144

Published by Distractions Ink
©Copyright 2017 by M. Meyers
A.K.A. Marcia Lynn McClure
Cover Photography by © Fotorince/Dreamstime.com
Cover Design and Interior Graphics by
Sandy Ann Allred/Timeless Allure

First Printed Edition: March 2017
First Hardcover Edition: March 2017

All character names and personalities in this
work of fiction are entirely fictional,
created solely in the imagination of the author.
Any resemblance to any person living or dead is coincidental.

McClure, Marcia Lynn, 1965—
The General's Ambition: a novella/by Marcia Lynn McClure.

ISBN: 978-0-9980595-3-2

Library of Congress Control Number: 2017938079

Printed in the United States of America

To Kristy Jo…

To old thrift store novels,
Rice Krispies treats for breakfast,
cashew clusters, and pralines.
But most of all…
To a friendship cherished in our memories
nestled warm in our hearts.
I miss you!

CHAPTER ONE

"Please tell me that you truly haven't done this, Father! Surely, you cannot actually have…have sold me to—"

"Hush, Renee. Of course I have not sold you!" the frail man interrupted. "I've simply arranged for you to be cared for."

Renee allowed the tears brimming in her lovely green eyes to escape. She brushed them from her cheeks with the back of her hands and determined to listen to her father's explanation—no matter how fraught with insanity it may seem.

The dying man forced a weak smile as he gazed at the vision of youth and beauty kneeling at his side. Tears of sorrow and fear spilled from Renee's emerald eyes. Her soft chestnut hair was escaping its worn scarlet ribbon. Yet the very existence of the ribbon gave the physician, Rudolph Millings, further assurance that he had arranged what was best for her. He reached up and affectionately caressed her flushed cheek. She was a unique beauty—even at only seventeen.

"You're so young, my child," her father said. "There is no doubt that you would be placed in an orphanage and then to servitude…and I will not die knowing you would be abandoned to such an existence." He paused as violent coughing wracked his ailing body. Renee wept as she waited for him to continue. After all, he was her father—and she was bound to his wishes. "This will serve, Renee," he said, at last. "Security, wealth…a solid lineage for the children you will someday bear."

"I beg you, Father…I do not want this," she whispered. "Please…better an orphanage than to marry without love."

"Hush now. It will come…for he is a good man."

"His father is a monster!" Renee exclaimed, however "He is notorious! I know you've heard the stories they tell in the village about his treachery, immorality…his violent nature! Surely you do not assume that I will be held safe in that place?"

"Even one so villainous as he would not dare lay hands on the wife of his only son, Renee. He values his son and his blood beyond all else…above all else…including his great wealth."

"Father, please…do not ask this of me," Renee pleaded through her tears.

"It is best, child," her father whispered. "I have been assured of it."

"By the honorable General Montan, no doubt," Renee breathed. She found her breath was labored—felt as if all the world were spinning and she had been thrown to the wind.

"No, my daughter…by his son, the young Roque Montan," her father said. "I am certain that this is right for you."

"Did you expect him to assure you otherwise, Father?" she asked.

"He is a good man, Renee. It is well I know him. He will—"

"Why, Father?" Renee interrupted as her sobbing increased. "Why would he approach you concerning me? What is the reason? We have no wealth, no great position in society."

"I love you, Renee," Rudolph Millings whispered.

"Know that I would not do anything to bring you to any harm. It is what is best." Renee watched as her father's eyes closed. "I must rest a moment," he mumbled.

Renee shook her head, knowing she had lost the battle. It was true then—she knew it was—illness had weakened her father's mind, rendered him somewhat mad.

The sudden and mad pounding at the door startled her from her despairing thoughts.

Her heart laden with grief, Renee called, "Just a moment." Unwillingly, she rose from her seat at her father's bedside and crossed the room. "One moment, please," she called, brushing more tears from her cheeks and smoothing her skirt.

Renee opened the door then, gasping when she saw none other than Roque Montan glaring down at her. The tall, handsome son of the infamous General Maurice Montan stood looming at the threshold, as wildly alluring as ever—tall, dark, and absurdly handsome. Yet in those moments, Renee knew only fear and trepidation in his presence.

"I have come to collect you," he stated.

"I am not a debt, sir," Renee responded, her teeth clenching with anguished indignation.

"I beg your pardon, Miss Millings," the man rather growled. "Let us say I have come to take you to my home then."

"I cannot go with you," she informed him. Lowering her voice, she added, "I will not leave while my father still draws breath."

Renee watched as Roque Montan glanced past her to where her father lay on his bed.

"I believe then…that the time has now arrived for you to come with me," he said.

Quickly Renee turned—looked to her father. Even for the distance, she could see her father's breath had stilled. His eyes were closed—his lips already bluing.

Shaking her head with horrified disbelief, with the agonizing pain of loss, Renee whispered, "He cannot be gone! He cannot have left me!" Frantic, she looked back to the tall man, looming in the doorway—he who would soon be her husband. "I cannot leave him," she explained as unendurable grief plunged into her heart.

"Very well. I will send for the new physician to attend you at once," Roque Montan stated. He then turned, striding away from the house.

"Oh, Father!" Renee cried. Tentatively she

approached him, hoping he had only fallen asleep. But alas, she had been a physician's daughter the entirety of her life; thus, she knew death at a mere glimpse.

Dropping to her knees, she flung herself across the body of her dead father. "Oh, Father! What misery have you sentenced me to?"

❧

Renee was struck mute as she entered the enormous ancestral home of the Montan family. She was too filled with grief and fear to take notice of the grandeur of the building and its lavish furnishings—too overcome with immeasurable loneliness to call upon the courage and independent nature that usually governed her.

Roque Montan had insisted that she accompany him to his home the moment that her father's body had been removed. She had taken a few moments to gather the things she felt she would need—though the man had assured her that her remaining belongings would follow her to his home within the next two days.

"You have acquired her then," General Maurice Montan bellowed, entering the room as the door closed, imprisoning Renee within the walls of her new home.

Renee cringed at the sight of the General—the man who was to be her father-in-law. He was considered handsome and boasted a magnificent military career, having fought gallantly in the war. Yet Renee knew he was a vile creature. Not only had she heard tales of his odious deeds, but every thread of her own instincts confirmed to her being that here before her stood a villain never before conquered.

The father was, indeed, the aged image of the son. The elder boasted graying at the temples and a less perfectly molded physique. Still, they were uncannily similar in appearance.

"I have brought her here, yes," Roque Montan answered with seeming indifference.

"Very well. Have Melba show her to her rooms…and I will see you in my study at once," the General ordered, striding past them.

Renee did not miss the heavy breath of frustration Roque Montan drew the moment the General had left the room. "I will bring Melba to you," he said to her. "Remain here," he ordered as he turned to leave her.

"Please, sir," Renee ventured.

The man halted but did not turn to face her.

With pure desperation, she continued, "I've a distant relation in a neighboring town. Please, let me go to her. You've no desire to follow through with this arrangement, I know. So I beg of you, sir—"

Turning to face her then, Roque Montan grumbled, "You are quite right. I would not involve myself in such a farce if I had any other venue before me." The anger and determination showing plain on his face caused Renee to step back from him as he spoke. "But seeing as my father has issued to me a forthright and unalterable ultimatum pertaining to…well, I have my reasons for adhering to his wishes."

"But why me, sir? There are so many others that are obviously more suitable. I am surely expendable in light of another," Renee pleaded.

Renee was startled as the man before her suddenly burst into a roar of laughter.

"You're completely innocent to the reasons why you were chosen, aren't you?" he asked.

Renee did not respond—only let her gaze fall to the immaculately polished wood floor beneath her feet. Her father had been wrong. It was an angry, hardened man standing before her—not a good man.

Her father had been wrong.

Roque Montan's amusement expired nearly as quickly as it had overcome him. "It's because my father fancies your most singular beauty," he told her. "With the aid of what he sees of his own handsome image manifest in myself...you will, no doubt, produce a strong and magnanimous child who will ensure the continuance of the Montan bloodline!"

Renee gasped.

As she looked up into the acrimonious expression of the man, he continued, "Your father was agreeable...with certain conditions arrived at between he and I alone. So fear not, little girl. You cannot be the unwilling recipient of my loathsome concupiscence for some time yet."

With one final indignant scowl, Roque Montan turned and marched away—leaving Renee alone in the great lonely space.

CHAPTER TWO

Roque Montan and Renee Millings were wed—a mere seven days following the burial of the physician Rudolph Millings. Renee had spent a dreadful, terrifying, and painfully forlorn week residing at the Montan estate previous to the ceremony. During that time, she experienced not only the brutal mourning of the loss of her father without a soul to comfort her but also a depth of anxiety and fear she could never before have imagined—for the General continually studied her. Whenever she was in his presence, Renee could not ignore, nor wish away, the expression of wanton lust ever present on his face.

General Maurice Montan's wife had died ten years before, and deep within her soul, Renee was certain the woman's death could only have been a truly merciful thing. The General was violent, frightening, and lustful. She pitied the poor woman who had borne this man's only son—the woman who had endured whatever ill-treatment he had seen fit to bestow upon her for the twelve long years she had spent in his house.

As the General was in constant perusal of her, his son no less than ignored her. Roque Montan seemed to prefer the pretense that she did not exist at all. He was not cruel to her, nor did he treat her with any disrespect. He simply seemed indifferent to her presence. In truth, this fact haunted Renee. He was to be her husband—her only ally in the world. Yet she drew no hope of comfort from him. And there was more—for Roque Montan was, though Renee tried to convince herself differently, an unparalleled male. He was tall, broad-shouldered, muscular, and insanely attractive! His eyes were an odd hue of jade green and his hair a blackish-brown boasting auburn streaks now and again. Strong jaw, high cheekbones, and a straight nose, accentuated by brilliantly white teeth, were other divine physical features he owned.

Since she had been a child, Renee had admired Roque Montan from afar. He had often visited her father when she was young, for treatment of various lacerations and a broken bone or two. Always he had remained silent when her father stitched a wound or set a bone—never uttering a complaint or exclamation of pain. She had often heard them talking together in lowered voices, making it impossible for her to discern the subject of the conversation they shared.

Roque Montan had even spoken to Renee on occasion. She specifically remembered one instance— when he had smiled at her and cheered away her sorrow. She had been twelve at the time and would never forget how her young heart had fluttered at receiving such a smile from one so gallant and handsome as he.

Renee had burst into her father's study one day several years previous, drowning in tears. A malicious playmate had torn Renee's favorite hair ribbon from her head and tossed it into a nearby puddle of mud.

"Not now, Renee," her father had scolded, as both he and his patient stood staring at her.

"But, Father," she cried, "that hateful Bernadette Sanders pulled my ribbon from my hair and destroyed it!" she cried.

"Momentarily, Renee. Sit outside the study please," her father firmly ordered.

Renee wiped the tears from her cheeks with the

back of her hands and obeyed. Several moments later, both men emerged from her father's study—and Roque Montan spoke to her.

Kneeling before her, the handsome young man asked, "We can't have your hair blowing about…now can we?"

Then—much to Renee's dismay—Roque Montan reached into his coat pocket and removed a length of scarlet ribbon. Extending his hand, he offered it to her.

"I know it's not the one you lost…but perhaps it will do for now, eh?" he asked, smiling at her.

Renee had hesitated, and he had taken her small hand in his, laying the ribbon on her upturned palm.

He cupped her chin in one strong hand, muttering, "No more tears now," as he wiped the tears from her cheeks with his thumb. "It distresses me to see such a lovely lady weeping." He had departed then, leaving Renee with the lovely scarlet treasure with which to tie up her hair.

As she stood watching the expressionless face of Roque Montan vowing fidelity and protection toward "this woman," Renee thought of the scarlet ribbon— the tattered red ribbon she had worn nearly every day for the past five years—the same ribbon she had safely tucked within the pages of her favorite book only that morning after removing it from her hair to replace it with the bridal veil she now wore.

"You may kiss the bride!" the curate announced.

The words quickly drew Renee's thoughts back to the present, and she felt the veil being lifted from her face. Roque Montan's penetrating glare rendered her breathless and trembling. Every manner of well-wishes erupted from the guests in attendance as his kiss lingered only a moment on her quivering lips. Yet to Renee, it seemed his kiss remained—for the sudden thrill erupting over her body at his touch did not immediately subside.

As the carriage lurched forward, Renee followed Roque Montan's promptings and waved to the crowd with polite smiles and nodding. Many had gathered outside the church to witness their departure, and Renee found such a crowd of onlookers only unsettled her further.

Yet once out of sight of the happy guests, Roque Montan's false smile faded. Thus, save the rhythmic trot of the horse, silence enveloped the carriage.

As they rode toward the Montan estate, Renee's thoughts only briefly lingered in self-pity, for she knew a sudden strange sort of pity for Roque Montan. After all, he too had been forced to marry one not of his own choosing.

"I am sorry that your father is such an appalling man," Renee said at last.

"I'm sure you are," he grumbled.

No other words passed between them.

When they arrived at the estate, it was to find the General awaiting their arrival.

"I see you've preceded us," Roque growled at the man in greeting.

"Ah, yes," the General said. He offered a lustful smile to Renee, causing a sense that her flesh was crawling to wash over her. "I wanted to make certain everything ensue with…efficiency."

"It is all of it my burden to bear now, General. You are relieved of your concerns," Roque growled. Renee gasped as he suddenly lifted her into the cradle his powerful arms and strode toward the staircase.

She was aware then of the man's uncommon strength, for he carried her as if he were hindered by no more than a cloth doll. She was bewildered, for she fancied she felt oddly secure in being carried by him.

Reflexively her arms clutched at his shoulders as

he carried her, and she felt inclined to utter a timorous, "I'm sorry."

Roque Montan's gaze locked with her own for an instant, but he made no acknowledgment of her apology.

"My dear boy," the General chuckled, causing Roque to pause his ascension, "if you consider this a burden to bear…why, if it weren't for my own face looking back at me now I might have cause to wonder at whether or not you are truly born of my blood."

Without giving response, Roque carried Renee up the remaining stairs and into a lavish bedchamber. Setting her to stand, he then closed the door behind them and locked the latch.

Renee glanced about the room, awed at the elegance of the furnishings. Her gaze fell to the enormous four-poster bed positioned very near to her—the only bed in the room. She looked to Roque in alarm, only to find him staring at her rather placidly.

His eyes smoldered with barely controlled anger and frustration as he growled in a voice tinged with fury, "Know this, wife: here, in this room, this very night…this marriage was consummated! Do you understand?"

"I-I beg your pardon, sir?" Renee stammered, overwhelmed with perplexity.

"I gave your father my oath," he continued, "my oath that I would not force you into submitting to me in order to produce my child until you reach the age of eighteen. I believe that is nearly ten months hence. This was an agreement between only your father and myself. The General has no notion of such conditions. His gaining a knowledge of it could induce him into contemplating or carrying out deeds of such perverse desperation that I'll not verbally utter them. For your safety and my own, we must reflect an image of having entirely sealed this marriage. Do you understand me? I fully intend to inherit all that is my father's in order that I may heal the heinous wounds he has inflicted upon our good name! To do so, I must appear to be attempting to further the existence of that name. I'm assuming that you are intelligent enough to comprehend what I am telling you?"

Renee nodded, though his words were blunt and shocking.

He continued, "He may question you. So, at the risk of corrupting your young mind, I ask...I assume that being a physician's daughter, you are educated in the process of human reproduction."

She was humiliated—blushed with the depths of her humiliations. Still, she bravely met his glare and nodded—for the instinct of self-preservation had begun to rekindle the strong attribute of independence in her character.

"Very well," he said. "Then if he questions you…you will not be too ignorant to reassure him." Roque's furious gaze bore through her to her very soul. He turned then and began pacing the room, yet undaunted in his instruction to her. "I am, by your own account, skilled and efficient in all husbandly duties," he stated.

When she was silent, he turned. She knew by the arch she felt of her brow that she wore an expression of skepticism. Yet she was not quick enough in masking it.

Angrily he took her chin in his hand and growled, "Do you doubt it?"

"No, sir," Renee muttered through clenched teeth.

He released her face and continued his instruction. "We will appear, whenever we find ourselves in the public eye, as any average newlywed couple. You will cease in referring to me as 'sir' and adopt my first name into your vocabulary. I will address you as Renee. Is this agreeable to you?"

Renee nodded. "Are you finished schooling me?" she asked.

"For the time being," he answered.

"Very well," Renee began, "and you will treat me with the utmost respect due a wife."

She was vexed by his assuming air of superiority. Furthermore, miraculously her courage—long absent in the face of her father's illness and death—was returning.

"Do not you dare to—" he began, glaring at her.

"I will not be your handmaiden, following you about as a weakling lamb!" she interrupted, however. "You will speak civilly to me at all times, you will not assume to order me about like a slave, and above all…" Renee's confidence faltered a moment. She looked up to him, pleading, "You will protect me…from your father."

Renee watched as the strength and anger seemed to drain from Roque Montan. He drew a deep breath, exhaling a heavy sigh. Closing his eyes, he began massaging his own temples.

"He will not touch you," he mumbled. "Even the

vilest creature would not dare to lay a hand on his only son's wife."

"There is one more thing," Renee ventured.

"What might that be?" Roque asked, frowning. It was obvious his head was paining him.

"You must pledge your absolute fidelity to me."

Roque's frown deepened, furrowing his handsome brow more deeply than Renee could have imagined possible. "I have done the very thing!" he growled. "Not more than one hour ago!"

"You married me, yes…promising to love, honor, and cherish me, as well," she reminded him. "And we both know you uttered a false pledge where those terms are concerned. I want your word here…now. Your promise of total adherence to faithfulness."

Angrily Roque took hold of Renee's arm. Through gritted teeth, he growled down at her, "I am an honorable man! No matter what the conditions of this arrangement…I would never endeavor to lead the life of depravity my father has. Do not assume you have married his reincarnation solely because I possess his physical features!"

"Very well," she whispered, wrenching her arm from his grasp. "But please do not be so easily vexed. It was, after all, a natural assumption." Renee almost grinned at the perplexed expression that crossed his face then. "Will I reside here, with you?" she asked, glancing about the room.

Roque sat—rather collapsed dejectedly on the bed. Renee knew it would take the mustering and exertion of an extraordinary amount of power to appear so commanding and in control as ever he did. She winced as sudden sympathy pricked heart.

"Yes," he sighed as he removed one boot. "You will sleep in my bed. It is large enough...and I will not touch you." He glared at her a moment. "And I expect the same courtesy from you, as well."

An odd shiver something akin to delight traveled the length of her spine. "Very well," she whispered as she watched him remove his other boot—then his shirt. Renee glanced away at the sight of his stripped, muscular torso.

"I cannot abide nightshirts," he grumbled. "They wrap 'round me like bindings."

"Well, surely you sleep in...in some manner of attire," Renee said.

"Not as a rule...but if you prefer..."

"I much prefer!" she exclaimed, breathless and with a profusion of crimson blush.

"There is a dressing screen in that corner...there,"

he grumbled, nodding toward the west corner of the room. He stood and began to unfasten his trousers.

Though she hoped she outwardly appeared to be calm, Renee wanted nothing more than to burst into tears! She wished she were twelve again—a young girl secreting a deep infatuation with a dashing young man named Roque Montan. Instead, she was married to him, knowing how fully he loathed her very presence. She was alone—ever so completely alone.

She took an extended amount of time changing into her nightdress. Her stomach ached with nausea, and her limbs trembled with apprehension. She wondered if the conditions placed upon Roque by her father were, in fact, a reality. If so, what if he decided not to honor them?

"Come along, girl," he growled from the other side of the screen. "Get on with it so we may both find some sleep."

With great anxiety, Renee stepped from behind the screen to stand at the foot of the bed.

Roque sat close to where she stood, dressed in a pair of worn-looking trousers.

"Will these suffice?" he asked.

"Yes. Thank you," Renee gulped, still unsettled by the sight of him bare from the waist up.

"Then let me bed you, girl. I'm done in," he said, standing and taking her shoulders in hand.

Forcefully—yet gently—he turned Renee, directing her to one side of the bed. Lifting the coverlets, he motioned for her to enter them. She did so—uncertain as to what else to do—and he covered her.

Renee clenched her eyes shut as she felt Roque's weight settle on the bed next to her. He exhaled a great sigh of fatigue, and in mere moments, it seemed, he breathing was slow and rhythmic.

Renee breathed with greater ease, for she realized that he must indeed have spoken the truth to her concerning his agreement with her father.

She lay awake for hours for fear that turning in her sleep would disturb the man sharing the bed. At long last, however, slumber was her companion, and she slept.

The sun shone brightly through the open shutters of the bedchamber. In the distance, a meadowlark's song heralded morning, and Renee smiled—her spirits lifted by the simple beauty of nature.

Inhaling deeply, Renee sighed—comfortable—contented. Yet her contentment was fleeting—for in the next moment she realized her head rested on one broad, bare shoulder belonging to Roque Montan. Gasping, she immediately raised—disturbing and waking him.

Roque's weary eyes opened but only to narrow slits. He lifted his head slightly from the pillow on which it rested.

"What?" he asked, looking to Renee.

"I'm so sorry, sir. Please, believe that I did not intend to disturb you," she rambled.

"What?" he asked—still incoherent.

"Just now, sir," she began, "I-I didn't meant to…"

"What? Oh. Oh. No matter," he stammered. "You were right to awaken me. Judging by the light, I far overslept," he said, pulling himself to a sitting position.

Gratefully, she realized he had not been aware of her diverting from his prior instruction of not touching him.

Renee was awestruck for a moment as she studied him. The smile returned to her face as she fancied how rather vulnerable and in complete disarray he appeared to be. His hair was tousled, hanging over his forehead and contributing greatly to his appealing appearance. Her fancy at his perhaps being less intimidating was cropped short, however, and she blushed as he clasped his hands behind his head, arching his back and thereby flaunting—though unintentionally—the perfect sculpture of his muscular torso.

"Well," he began, yawning, "how shall we while away the hours today, wife?"

Entirely unsettled, Renee stood from the bed and hurried toward one window. "It is such a lovely day, isn't it?"

"We could stay in this very room and pretend to be the impassioned newlyweds," he suggested. "Or…we could play at cards. Perhaps poker. Do you play?"

"No. Not poker, at least," she answered. "I've never heard of that game."

"Well, then I shall have to teach you," he said, yawning and stretching once more. "We will have to entertain ourselves for hours on end by some means. Don't you agree?"

"Yes, sir," she responded.

"Or…I suppose we could invite the General in for a friendly chat, if you wish. I wouldn't be surprised to find that he's bored peepholes in the walls throughout this room." He chuckled as Renee began intently studying the walls. "I'm in jest, girl."

Renee was chagrinned at having been found so gullible. Her pride flared, and she spun around, glaring at him. "If you would allow it, Roque...I believe I would like to visit the cemetery," she said. "I've haven't had the chance to look after my father's grave since you acquired me last week."

"Look after it? It seems hardly likely that anything..." he began. He paused, his eyes narrowing with curiosity. Renee was astonished when he said then, "As you wish. We shall go together." He glanced away, adding, "But much later in the week. Appearances, after all."

Renee thought her heart had fallen to take up residence in the pit of her stomach. She had wanted to visit her father alone—to talk to him. Not that he could answer her, of course—but she longed to visit his resting place.

As if having read her thoughts, Roque assured her, "Fear not, my frightened little field mouse. You shall be able to visit him alone soon enough."

Renee was distracted from her heartache for a moment then—enchanted as she studied him once more. Roque Montan appeared so less threatening in his present state that she realized she was not as fearful in his presence as she had been even the very day before.

"Why do you smile so amusedly at me?" he thundered, frowning.

"You are much less terrifying at first light," she courageously admitted, stepping behind the dressing screen.

"Do not replace your nightdress as of yet," he ordered, unexpectedly appearing beside her. "I know well the General. He will have breakfast brought up at any moment, and it is best that you look as if you have been...shall we say mauled...so that Melba may report back to him."

"Surely you exaggerate...don't you?" Renee asked.

"About what?" he asked in return. Reaching out, he pulled the scarlet ribbon from Renee's hair. As her hair cascaded over her shoulders, she shyly glanced away. Oh, how she hoped he did not recognize the tattered adornment.

"About the General," he began. "He is truly obsessed with obtaining an assured lineage."

"He is?"

Roque studied the ribbon for a moment. Fearful

he would indeed recognize it as the same he had gifted her years before, Renee snatched it from his hand.

There came a soft knocking the door then.

"Are we expected to have heard that?" Renee whispered.

"Most intentionally not, I am sure," Roque answered.

Renee watched then, mesmerized as a mischievous grin flattered Roque's handsome face.

"Come along," he said. "We'll put his fevered mind at ease." And taking her hand, he led her to the bed once again. "Quickly. You have played at possum before, haven't you?" he asked, his smile broadening.

"Of course," Renee answered, giggling softly as she crawled beneath the coverlets once more.

"Sshh. Give no appearance of mischief," Roque whispered as he joined her in the bedding.

Renee closed her eyes, determined to play the farce to the fullest. She gasped, however, her eyes opening wide as she felt Roque's arms about her—as he embraced her unexpectedly in his powerful arms.

"Sshh," he commanded as he pulled her body against his own. Renee was entirely unnerved at having her face placed flush to his bare chest. She could smell the enticing aroma of his skin—was astounded at the softness of it. She had imagined he would feel rough and cold somehow. But as she heard the door being unlocked from the outside, she closed her eyes and attempted to mimic the slow breathing induced by sleep.

She could discern whispering and determined it must be Melba, the housekeeper, and the General discussing the success of his endeavors.

"How dare you intrude!" Roque roared. Releasing Renee, he sat up, glaring at the intruders.

Renee looked toward the door to find the General and Melba indeed stood within the room.

"Have you not the courtesy, nor decency, to knock before entering?" Roque shouted, still sitting up in the bed.

"We did knock," the General answered as Melba stood looking from father to son awash in intimidation and guilt.

"With a feather duster, no doubt," Roque accused, leaving the bed and striding to stand before his father. "Now, get out! We do not wish to be disturbed. I see you didn't even have the foresight to arrive with the excuse of bringing breakfast in."

Renee saw that, indeed, Melba held no breakfast

tray in her trembling hands.

"Mind your tongue, boy," the General growled as he turned to leave. "I am still master in this house."

"Yes. But I am the bridegroom in it," Roque said as the General paused before exiting.

"I'm sorry, sir," Melba whispered. "Ma'am," she added, nodding to Renee.

Renee felt pity for the woman, for she was obviously ashamed of being a participant in the intrusion.

"I understand, Melba. Do not worry yourself over it," Roque said as he closed the door behind her, locking it once again. "I most certainly will have these locks changed," he added, turning to look at Renee.

"Most certainly, lest they interrupt my poker instruction," Renee said. She was suddenly amused—entirely amused by the utter absurdity of the situation. She struggled to stifle a giggle.

Roque chuckled as well, and his smile was pure dazzling. "Let us begin said instruction then. I've suddenly no doubt you will eventually prove formidable competition."

Thus, Renee Montan's first full day of marriage was spent (as were the two to follow) in learning the varied attributes of poker.

CHAPTER THREE

After three days of being sequestered in their bedchamber—Roque teaching Renee the fine art of poker in a manner befitting a true gentleman—Roque had finally relented to allow them to be seen out and about. The cemetery was little more than two miles from the Montan estate, and as Roque accompanied Renee on her quest to visit her father's grave, Renee was grateful for the fresh air, the sun, and Roque's presence.

She had found her husband was, in truth, a vastly dissimilar variety from his father. Roque could be extremely pleasant—involve himself in conversations fraught with humor as well as significance. She had also begun to sense he would, indeed, shield her from any harm—for whether or not he cared a wit for her, he was honorable, and she was, by law, his wife.

As they reached the gates of the cemetery, Roque paused to purchase a bouquet of cut flowers from a vender.

"Thank you," Renee said as Roque handed the blossoms to her.

"I'll wait here for you," he stated, gesturing she should proceed without him.

Grateful for his understanding her need for solitude, she smiled at him—nodded. She wandered among the tombstones until she found the yet fresh grave where her father's mortal remains lay at rest. Kneeling, she placed the flowers at the base of the large granite stone engravened with her father's name. Tenderly she traced the letters of his epitaph with her fingers.

"What shall I do, Father?" she whispered. "I'm so terribly in love with him, you know. I've only just this moment admitted it to my ownself. Roque cares nothing for me, Father! Do you know how we've spent our first days of marriage? Do you? Playing at poker in our bedchamber." She paused, brushing tears from her cheeks—tears for her father—tears for Roque.

"He smiles often," she continued. "Smiles at things I say. But I wonder…does he smile out of

34

sheer amusement at my ignorance or because he finds me slightly clever at times? And I'm so terribly afraid of his father! I've never seen such evil intentions apparent in human eyes."

Renee contented herself for several more minutes with revealing the thoughts and feelings of her heart. Then she rose and returned to where Roque stood waiting.

He nodded with apparent sympathy as she approached, and she smiled at him. Renee fancied he appeared very much as some handsome guardian angel in those moments.

"Hello, Roque," a voice said.

The couple turned, and Renee was immediately piqued at the sight of Bernadette Sanders standing before them, smiling bewitchingly at Roque. Bernadette Sanders—the same intolerable Bernadette Sanders who had stolen Renee's hair ribbon so many years before. Renee knew (as did everyone else in town) that Bernadette had cherished the knowledge that she would eventually find her way into receiving a proposal from Roque Montan. Furthermore, Renee also knew (as did everyone else) that Bernadette Sanders was the only young woman in town to ever have actually held the man's attention for any length of time. It had been rumored not more than a year previous that Roque had paid court to her for a brief occasion.

"Bernadette," Roque greeted.

"And just look at you, Renee," the young woman chimed with a sweetness in intonation paralleling that of a poisoned apple. "Been to see your dear father, I see."

Renee was suddenly exceedingly aware of her own appearance—in particular the no doubt red, swollen state of her eyes caused from weeping over her father's grave. She only nodded in response, dropping her gaze—humiliated to be found in such an emotional state by Bernadette Sanders.

"I cannot believe you've gone and gotten married, Roque, darling," Bernadette rather whined. "I'm heartbroken, you know."

"Oh, I'm certain you are," Roque said, smiling at the young woman.

Yet when he said nothing to further engage her in conversation, Bernadette politely excused herself. "Well, I guess I'll be off. You two have a lovely day." She paused, and Renee recognized the malice in her bright eyes. "But I hope you do find some other thing to do together other than visiting the dead…

something more befitting the blissful state of being newly wed."

Tossing her head in a manner of triumph, Bernadette giggled and walked away.

Inwardly, Renee seethed with indignity. The woman was intolerable!

"Raise your head, girl!" Roque growled in a whisper.

Startled by his command, Renee looked up to him with inquiry.

His scowl deeply furrowed his brow, and she could not fathom why he appeared so suddenly vexed.

"Do not let her mock and intimidate you in such manner," he explained. "You are perfectly warranted in grieving after your father."

Renee wiped the tears from her cheeks. "I've always detested that woman," she confessed in a whisper.

"Well, you're my wife now," he said. "And at the risk of appearing awash with vanity…you now possess something that she never could…that something being me. Therefore, flaunt it over her, if you will. But never drop your gaze before her. It's cowardly."

"I am not a coward!" Renee argued with defiance.

"Then do not drop your gaze from her! Meet her glare for glare."

He took her arm and linked it through his own. "Come along now. I've got a matter to discuss with…someone in town. You may amuse yourself at the mercantile," he said as he began leading her toward the township.

❧

"Everyone knows he only married her because the General wants a grandson that's as handsome as himself."

Renee stood to one side of the mercantile feigning an interest in a bolt of cloth. Yet the hushed whispering of the cluster of leathery old gossips huddled in the opposite corner of the place easily reached her ears.

"I wager he's as brutal as his father," one woman said.

"No. He's the saint in the family, that one. He'll brush the dirt from that name eventually," another countered.

"Poor little thing…expected to bear children at such a tender age," another gossip sympathized.

In that moment, Renee was thankful her father

had thought to arrange terms with Roque—for the whispering and speculation would cease eventually as it became apparent that the new Mrs. Roque Montan would not be presenting her husband with an heir anytime in the near future. Still, their gossiping stung her pride.

"Oh, there you are, my darling."

At the sound of his voice, Renee turned to see Roque striding toward her—a happy smile marking his countenance.

"Roque?" she asked, puzzled by his blissful appearance.

"Yes," he answered. "I've finished my errand. Are you ready to return home with me, mouse?"

"Y-yes," Renee stammered, nodding at him. She frowned, however, entirely puzzled by his rather excess delight.

Roque took her arm, linking it through his own. Placing a kiss to her forehead, he led her through the mercantile toward the door.

"Ladies," he greeted the rather covenish-looking assembly of old women. With a bow vaunting a mastery of well-mannered propriety, Roque tipped his hat as they passed the conglomeration of meddlers lingering near the door.

He paused and turned back to them, offering a generous smile. "Isn't she a beauty, ladies?" he inquired.

"Oh, yes, sir!" and, "Lovely, Mr. Montan! Just beautiful!" came the replies of passionate agreement.

"What lovely children the two of you will have, sir," one woman said, smiling.

Roque chuckled, "Oh! I hope to have her all to myself for some time yet. I'm a selfish man, you understand." He conspiratorially winked at the withered old woman.

Renee giggled as numerous sets of graying and overly thick eyebrows arched in astonished realization.

"You'll excuse us, won't you, ladies?" Roque said, bowing to them. "I feel I've shared her long enough for one day."

Renee heard the dismayed whispers erupting among the collection of old women as she and Roque walked away.

"They're still prattling," Renee giggled.

"Are they now?" Roque said. He paused and took her by the shoulders, turning her to face him. "Well then, let's drop them dead where they stand with a brazen act of impropriety," he muttered as he pulled

Renee's body against his own—his mouth seizing hers in a deep and seemingly ardent kiss.

Roque's kiss instantly rendered her breathless and weak. Renee could well imagine a tornado was growing within her bosom—filling her lungs with superfluous air.

All too quickly, Roque ended the kiss, gazing down at her with the light of victory in his eyes.

"What are you doing?" Renee exclaimed in a whisper. She glanced back to find the nest of old women gasping, clutching at their bosoms, feigning astonished disapproval at the improper display they had just witnessed.

"Schooling the people in this town that they dare not speculate where my personal life is concerned," Roque growled. "Now, cease in looking so disturbed," he commanded. "They'll think we are insincere in our affections."

Renee glared up at him with riled indignation. "You don't want them speculating…is that it?" she asked.

Roque inhaled a deep breath and straightened his collar. "Exactly."

"Very well," she muttered.

Before Renee could further contemplate her

capricious gesture, she reached up, pulling Roque's head to meet her own—applying a thorough kiss to his alluring mouth.

Taking her face between strong hands, Roque held her from him, glaring at her with his own indignation.

"Two can play at this as well as at poker, Roque," Renee whispered triumphantly.

"That is true," he mumbled. "However...in any contest there can be only one victor."

Renee gasped as Roque's capable mouth overwhelmed hers once more. Weak and rendered dizzy by the bliss bathing her, she gripped his powerful forearms for support as he took her face between his hands—owned her very essence with his kiss.

"There now," he said, finally ending their exchange. "They'll be swooning if we stand here engaged as we are any longer." He arched one eyebrow as Renee swayed upon his releasing her. "Furthermore, your vexation at my impertinence may send you foundering as well if we don't commence with a steady gait."

Renee was ever so grateful that he had mistaken the elation she was feeling derived of his kiss for annoyance at his behavior. She accepted his offered arm, forcing her liquefying knees to propel her forward.

"Withered-up, interfering old prunes," Roque muttered as they walked. "That will give them something to talk about."

"They're merely lonely creatures with nothing better to do with what little vigor is left to them," Renee defended, attempting to fan the blush from her cheeks with her hand.

"Campaigning for sainthood today, Renee?" Roque mumbled, obviously scornful of her vindicating the old women.

"Why not?" she asked. "My character has already been compromised this day. I may as well promote someone else's."

"Initiating amorous gestures with one's spouse does not discredit one's character, Renee," he stated. "And, before you accuse me further, my oath to your father encompassed only the act of—"

"Yes, yes, yes!" Renee interrupted, not wanting him to verbalize the issue. "I know. I know."

Roque was undaunted, however. "As I was saying—and by the way, it is profoundly discourteous to interrupt—my affirmation to your father included only…rather, for the sake of your tender ears, did not incorporate all other aspects of physical affections."

Renee cleared her throat, attempting to salvage a shred of dignity. "Well, do not expect that you may take whatever liberties you please at any given time," she warned.

Roque chuckled. "Do not try to convince me you're regretful in the least for sending those old gossips into fits of frenzy. I'm beginning to know you, Renee. Three days locked in one room playing poker…well, let us just say we've gotten to know each other in a most intimate manner. You are as unconventional as I, whether or not you will openly admit it." He laughed wholeheartedly then. "Just think what a vision! Those five old crones darting about town, spreading the word to every available ear that Roque Montan was most assuredly not forced into marriage with the late physician's daughter." He paused, and Renee watched as an enormous smile brightened his face. "Nor—judging from your reaction, to which they were privy—was she forced to marry him."

Renee's mouth fell agape in astonishment—for he was indeed correct! She had publicly seized upon him, unashamedly kissing him.

"Come now, Renee," he said, slapping her on the back as he might a chum. "Chin up! You can be assured that after today, Bernadette Sanders will no longer speak in such a condescending manner to you."

It was true—and Renee sighed as resignation won her.

❧

"It reaches my ecstatic self that the two of you are getting along most agreeably," the General said. Renee's appetite evaporated at the sound of the General's voice as he entered the dining room. "I hear you've been visiting in town, as it were, this very afternoon…and together."

The General chuckled, an utter air of triumph about him. "Well done, my girl," he said, looking to Renee. His smile was vile. "I feared that I had perhaps been overconfident in your…attributes…in your being able to crumble my son's pledge not to…not to take a wife until I was in the grave."

"General Montan," Renee began, "you will please refrain from discussing these matters with me. They are of a personal nature, and I deem them as definitively private."

The General's eyes narrowed; his smile

broadened. Lowering his voice, he said, "There's no need for reticence, my girl. Roque is, fortunately, endowed with many of my own charming attributes. No doubt his competency in these 'matters,' as you call them, is unparalleled as well."

Renee startled as Roque slammed his fist on the table and stood—enraged. "We are attempting to nourish ourselves. Do not spoil our appetites, General," he growled. Renee noted that his fists trembled with restrained fury.

The General chuckled again, however. "Very well. We most definitely want to keep you both strong and healthy. Don't we, Roque?"

"Do not provoke me further, General," Roque threatened through clenched teeth.

The General looked from his son to Renee and back. Without another word, he left the room.

Roque collapsed into his chair—shoved his plate away from him to the center of the table. Looking to Renee, he said, "You must learn to ignore his brutish innuendoes. They will only increase, and you mustn't let the General rankle you so."

"You can't even refer to him as your father, can you?" Renee observed aloud.

"Could you?" he asked, glaring at her.

"No," she admitted. "He sets my skin to crawling."

"Resign yourself to familiarity with that particular sensation," Roque said. "For it will not cease simply because he is out of the room for the moment. Knowing he is in the house is enough for me." He stood then and marched from the room.

CHAPTER FOUR

The days turned into weeks and the weeks into months—six months. For six months, Renee lingered in sensing the General's impatience with waiting for the announcement of an impending birth of an heir. For six months, Renee was assured that Roque had not the least intention, or desire, to begin some sort of conjugal relationship with her. She had managed to convince herself he valued her as a friend at least—an amusing companion. Yet she more often felt she was an anchor of sorts—something that kept him bound to his father's detestable presence.

Late one night, Renee awoke to angry voices steeped in argument. When she found that Roque was no longer in the bed with her, she lit a candle and quietly crept downstairs in the direction from whence the voices drifted. There she found the library door ajar, a dim light emanating from it.

"You repulse me!" It was Roque.

"And I find you repugnant!" the General countered. "The girl is beautiful! She's been in your bed for six months…and still there's no indication that—"

"Nor will there be!" Roque growled. "And for a greater length of time than you can know!"

"Why?" the General asked. Renee fancied the question had a ring of panic. "Is she flawed? Is there something of which her father did not tell you? If you have been deceived into marrying her, boy, we will seek annulment immediately."

As Renee peered into the library, Roque laughed in disbelief. "I? Deceived into marrying her? We both of us know what a hypocritical notion that is! Of course there is no flaw in her. She is perfect. Perfect! You…you are so audacious! You thought you could force me into sequentially having her wed, bedded, and bred!"

"I never stipulated the sequence, Roque," the General taunted.

Renee grimaced at the conversation's crudity—as Roque continued to vent his fury and frustration on his father.

"Well, fool that you are…believe it when I tell you that I and I alone ultimately have control over my own life!" Roque's laughter caused Renee to worry for his sanity a moment. "I bartered with her father," he informed the General, "bartered before he died, vowing not to force his daughter into submitting to me before her eighteenth birthday."

Renee watched as the General's face grew vermilion and distended with his heightening wrath.

"So, you see, General," Roque continued, exhaling a sigh of triumph, "I've kept you waiting… waiting for something that there is no possible hope of obtaining for at least four more months."

"Do you mean to tell me," the General seethed, "that you have not moved to touch her?"

"Oh, this you can believe. I've touched her…and it is no easy chore to keep from thoroughly ravaging her at times. But my loathing for you will keep me from it still. For I—though it must be my mother's blood pumping my heart—am an honorable man."

"An honorable man?" the General roared. "You are a fool, boy!" The General turned and walked toward the hearth. He paused—stared into the flames therein a moment. "Very well," he began at last. "Bernadette Sanders. She has always fancied you.

Father her child then, and we will legitimize it."

Renee's hand flew to her mouth, her stomach twisting with nausea.

Will Roque agree? she wondered. No! Roque was the honorable man she knew him to be. She did know him to be honorable—nearly above all else!

"You," Roque breathed with visible loathing. "You afflict me with your mere presence in this room."

The General chuckled. "Why, Roque, my boy. The very words your mother once said to me…the night you were conceived."

Renee screamed as Roque lunged at his father, striking him brutally across the jaw with his fist. Rushing into the room, she took hold of his powerful arm before he could administer another blow—another perhaps more lethal blow. She watched as the General stood, wiping the blood from his mouth.

"I'll give you that, Roque…for slandering your mother," the General mumbled. Yet he smiled next, and Renee fancied he was actually proud somehow of provoking his son to wrathful violence.

The loathsome General turned his attention to Renee then. "I now see the great strain Roque is enduring, my dear."

Roque wrenched his massive arm from Renee's grasp and turned to leave the room.

Yet the General continued, "He's never known you, is that it? It is no wonder he is so ill-tempered." Renee glared at the villain as he continued, "Do you know what a struggle it must be on him...spending night after sleepless night with you there...scantily clad and so tempting in his bed?"

"You will silence yourself at once!" Roque roared. As he aggressed upon his father once more, Renee stepped between them.

"He sleeps peacefully enough," Renee stated.

"He only simulates peaceful sleep, my dear," the General chuckled. "Why not let me escort you to your chamber this evening? I assure you that—"

"Secure your foulsome mouth!" Roque shouted, lunging at his father. Renee took hold of his arm to stall him. "If you touch her..." Roque threatened, pointing a trembling index finger at the General, "you touch her...and I will kill you. Make no mistake of that promise."

Rather violently, Roque scooped Renee into his arms, striding from the room—the General's malicious laughter echoing after them.

Once inside their bedchamber, Roque rather

indecorously deposited Renee carelessly on the bed and began pacing the floor.

"He cannot be allowed to win," he mumbled to himself. "I cannot let him best me."

Renee tried to steady her anxious breathing. In that moment, she knew she was on the precipice of catastrophe—from one venue or another.

Inhaling a deep breath in an effort to calm herself, she considered all she had heard. Then, with her wits about her once more—with the understanding of how determined the General was to see his progeny continue—she said, "I will bear your child. Then he will cease in tormenting you."

Roque looked at her, his mouth agape in astonishment. A deep frown furrowed his brow as he breathed, "What did you say?"

"It's all very simple. Don't you see?" Renee answered. "He won't badger you then. He wouldn't threaten you anymore."

"I do see," he said. "I really do." His eyes narrowed. "You're willing to make the ultimate sacrifice and permit me to…well, I suppose the ultimate sacrifice would be submitting to the General. Therefore submitting to me would be slightly less than the ultimate—"

Roque was silenced as the sharp sting of Renee's slap heated his cheek.

"How dare you mock me!" she cried, tears springing to her eyes.

Roque sighed—raked a trembling hand through his hair. "Forgive me," he said. "I am fatigued and angry and feeling as if forfeit is inevitable."

Renee held her breath as he gently took her hand, placing a warm kiss to the back of it. "You are the pawn in a brutal game of war. You do not deserve to be treated with such a lack of tenderness. I am truly wretched, am I not?" He sighed once more and smiled at her—though she knew it was feigned. "Come along to bed. Things are never as bleak in the light of day, are they, Renee?"

Renee crept along the corridor, silent and unbelieving that she had been awakened by voices yet again. Once more she had found Roque absent from their bed and feared that another confrontation might erupt between him and the General.

These voices were hushed—not raised in anger. They emanated from a room near Melba's. As Renee approached the door from whence light shone beneath, she clutched at her stomach, for instantly she recognized the voices: the voices of Roque and Bernadette Sanders. She could never mistake Roque's voice, for it echoed in her mind—was dearer to her than any other sound on earth. Neither could she ever mistake the voice of Bernadette Sanders, for too many were the times it had taunted her.

Renee pushed the door open and gasped at the sight before her. She felt as if a serpent had wound about her heart—constricting—driving the very life from her! There they stood, Roque clad in only the trousers in which he slept, Bernadette in a gossamer nightdress. Roque held Bernadette in his arms, gazing into her face with longing. As the candle slipped from Renee's hand and fell to the floor, Bernadette turned.

"Oh dear, Roque. It seems your wife has found us out," the poisonous woman said. She laughed then, pulling herself more snuggly into Roque's embrace.

"Roque? No!" Renee stammered, barely able to draw breath for the pain in her bosom. "I said I would…that I would willingly…that I would gladly…"

Roque arched a curious brow. "But I never wanted you, Renee. Surely you realize that by now. I only married you because the General ordered me to."

Renee put her hands to her ears to block out his cruel words. "Roque!" she cried. "Please do not say this to me! Please!"

"Renee? Renee! You're dreaming."

Renee's eyes drifted open. She saw Roque's boyishly tousled hair—his handsome, rugged face gazing down on her. Quickly, she glanced about.

"Did you send her away?" she asked, confused.

"Who?" he asked.

"Bernadette!" she cried, tears spilling from her eyes to streaming over her cheeks. "Your lover!"

Roque smiled—then frowned. "What?" he exclaimed. "I have no lover, and well you know it. Now sit up. You're still dreaming."

Renee did as he instructed, brushing tears from her cheeks and glancing about to ensure Bernadette Sanders was not in the room.

"Now, tell me…what sort of ridiculous dreams are these?" he asked, yawning.

"None. I'm sorry I disturbed you," Renee answered, lying back down.

"Oh, no. No, indeed," he chuckled. "You awaken me by screeching my name, tears streaming over your cheeks, and then accuse me of having a lover…

Bernadette Sanders, at that. You will elucidate now, Renee."

Renee looked up to him. "You would never do such a thing as to father her child, would you?" she asked.

"What? Who?" he asked. She saw sudden understanding wash over him then, and he exclaimed, "No! Of course not!"

"Y-you pledged fidelity, Roque…" Renee began in a whisper.

"I did. And I am scrupulous, Renee," he told her. "I am not the General. I own great restraint and strength of will. If that is what haunts your dreams, then put it to bed with the rest of you each night."

"I have your word?" she asked, searching his expression for visible reassurance.

He sighed and rolled his eyes with exasperation. "Yes," he confirmed. Placing a hand to his chest where beneath his heart resided, he added, "My word as a gentleman."

Renee sighed—smiled with sudden respite. Some reflex she could not thwart caused her hand to reach up to run her fingers through his tousled hair.

Roque grinned. He took her hand from his hair, lacing his fingers with her own.

"Does it feel as you imagined it would?" he asked—a teasing, mischievous smile curving his lips.

Renee dropped her gaze. "I never imagined what it would feel like," she lied.

His fingers tightened on her own. "Liar," he chuckled.

Renee met his smile with defiance—though she knew she had lied. Further, she knew herself to be at the greater disadvantage, for she lay flat on her back, and he was propped on one elbow, hovering over her.

"For discourteously interrupting my slumber, I'm going to confiscate sentiments from your lips now, Renee," he whispered.

"What?" she gasped.

"I might make to mention that I mean to collect them in the form of kisses and not as a verbal apology." Her eyes widened in dismay as he chuckled. "It's the least I should receive after being awakened in such a discourteous manner. Don't you agree?"

"I-I…" Renee stammered.

With a husky chuckle, Roque pressed a teasing kiss to one corner of her mouth.

"It is a thoroughly unfounded concern, Renee," he whispered, brushing the hair from her cheek. "I am an estimable man and a faithful husband."

"I know," she whispered.

"The General will try to introduce doubt into your mind at every turn…as you have witnessed tonight."

She nodded.

"Trust in me," he whispered, his lips lightly brushing hers.

His massive form was suddenly flush with hers as his kiss became moist and demanding. Renee let her hands travel over his broad shoulders to the back of his neck, to be lost in the softness of his hair.

With one final, hunger-driven play at her mouth, Roque broke from her. Inhaling a long, deep breath, he rolled to his back and exhaled a heavy sigh.

"I am a man, however, Renee," he reminded.

"I know," she whispered.

"No more bad dreams, agreed?" he asked, turning from her and tugging at the coverlet.

"Yes. Agreed."

She smiled when she heard him whisper to himself, "Bernadette Sanders? I thought you at least credited me with good taste."

Renee wished the General did not exist—that she and Roque could somehow find happiness together.

Yet if the General did not exist, there would be no magnificent Roque. She smiled once more, for at least the General had one commendation to his existence on the earth: his son.

"I have gained control of my temper once more," the General announced as he intruded on Roque and Renee's breakfast the following morning. "Having at first seethed upon the information you disclosed to me last night, Roque," he continued, "I see now that the girl's father may have had concerns about leaving his only daughter in the hands of one such as you…one with a sire owning the reputation yours does. Therefore, I forgive you both for your deceitfulness. Am I to understand, Renee, that in four months' time, you will have reached your eighteenth anniversary?"

Renee straightened her posture and determined to appear composed. "Yes," she answered.

"Then I'll not have to wait much longer, will I?"

Renee looked to Roque as she heard him draw a deep breath. "The fact remains, however," Roque began, "that this…this issue…is still of a very private nature. Thus, Renee and I will decide if—"

"No!" the General roared. "You will not decide,

boy! I'll no longer tolerate these deceptions…these schemes!" He was enraged, and Renee trembled as he continued with his ranting. "Know this, Roque. You threatened to kill me for touching her, did you not? Well, I now return the possible peril upon you! This girl will bear my lineage! If not by your own hand…then by mine!"

With calm intonation and demeanor, Roque simply said, "Dare to attempt it…and you will die."

"Meddle further, boy…and you will!" the General growled. He turned, exiting the room.

Renee sat staring at Roque as he coolly recommenced with consuming his breakfast.

"I'm not a puppet, Roque," she ventured.

"You are in his eyes," he said. "An instrument with which to provide himself with assured progeny."

"And to you? What am I to you in this?" she cried, slamming her tender fist on the table and ejecting herself from her chair. "Only a weapon to wield against him…to enrage and provoke the father you have come to loathe so completely!" Renee sensed the panic rising within her. Hastening to where Roque sat, she knelt on the floor beside him, pleading, "Please, Roque…send me away. Cannot you see that he is sincere in his threats?"

Roque continued to look at the victuals before him as he said, "He is sincere, Renee...as am I. He would have to kill me before I would allow him to touch you."

Renee slowly rose to her feet—watched as he began eating once more. "You're as obsessed as he is...obsessed with winning...with thwarting his plans," she said. "That's it, isn't it? It has nothing to do with the agreement between you and my father, does it? You only want to ensure that your father does not prevail."

"That's not true," he began, looking to her at last.

"Yes, it is," she interrupted as her heart began splintering into painful fragments. "I see it all so clearly now. You spoke to my father first. That's the only reason—"

"Stop this," he growled, rising and glaring at her. "Do not accuse me of using his tactics, Renee. You don't perceive every circumstance. You assume that you do, but you don't. So cease the feigning of possessing a wisdom that is not yours."

"Then endow me with a complete knowledge, Roque. I surely deserve no less than that!" she cried. "I am the victim in this dispute between the two of you! Surely I deserve to know—"

Roque took her arm. His teeth were clenched, his voice barely above a whisper as he leaned forward and said, "This knowledge I will give you, Renee. In four months' time…the agreement I made with your father will be met. So prepare yourself, mouse…for the very hour of your eighteenth year, I will meet the finish of that accursed oath with the greatest of pleasure. I shall be free of it, and you will no longer have cause to fear insult from the General." Throwing his napkin to the table, he stormed away.

"I doubt you even know the day of my birth, let alone the hour," Renee muttered to herself.

She was startled when Roque turned and strode to her once more.

Cocking his head to one side, he smiled a smile of contented superiority. "Trust in this, mouse. Your father gifted me a cognizance of the very minute!" Wagging a warning forefinger at her, he added, "Prepare yourself, wife—for my patience is near spent!"

CHAPTER FIVE

Two more months passed without great incident. Renee had nearly begun to believe that the General had resigned himself to waiting and abiding by his son's conditions. He had ceased his references of the conception of another Montan heir, and he and Roque seemed to tolerate one another for the most part.

Renee wondered why Roque endured such circumstances. He was not a weak man by any means. Rather, he was superior to most in his strength and determined independence, as well as in his physical attributes. There had to be more—more than just a desire to usurp his father's will. Thus, as she often did, she was deep in thoughtful pondering of the situation as she left the cemetery one morning after having tended to her father's grave.

The air was cold, for snow had fallen the night before. She turned and directed herself toward the mercantile, intending to purchase a pair of warmer stockings. The sudden change in the weather had left her ill-prepared with a lack of proper clothing.

Upon entering the establishment, she noticed an immediate hush fell over the familiar coven of meddlers standing near the threshold.

"Good morning, ladies," Renee offered as she removed her mittens. She cheerfully smiled at the women.

The women each greeted her in return, yet she felt they appeared somewhat sheepish in their manner. One by one the women began to look—rather guiltily—to the other side of the room. Renee allowed her own gaze to trail those of the elderly gossips. The sight that met her caused her knees to buckle.

There, standing before one of the glass cases housing jewelry and more expensive items stocked by the store, was Roque—Bernadette Sanders at his side. They were leaning over the case studying something cached within. Bernadette giddily giggled and affectionately linked her arm through Roque's.

Renee glanced back to the group of women, all of whom now wore arched eyebrows and expectant expressions. Renee was being baited—and she lunged.

"Well! Bernadette! Roque!" she chirped. "Whatever brings you two out on such a chilly day?"

Roque swung around, all hue draining from his face as he looked at his rosy-cheeked wife.

"Ah! What a shame, Renee," Bernadette whined, pursing her lower lip. "Now you've spoiled everything!"

Renee loathed the flaxen-haired beauty. "I'm sure I have. Only, what is it I've spoiled?" she asked. Every inch of her body was trembling with hurt and humiliation as she stared at the couple before her.

Roque stood still, as if etched in stone, attempting no explanation.

Therefore, Bernadette spoke once more. "Why, your birthday present, of course."

"Really? How thoughtless of me," Renee sighed, walking to meet them and peering down into the case. "Let me see," she mused, "the diamond stickpin perhaps?" She looked up, but Roque only continued to stare in the opposite direction. She did not miss the rising expression of indignation on his face, however. "No, no, no. Here it is! Of course! A ruby initial brooch. Oh, and there are several from which to choose." She dropped her voice so that only Roque and Bernadette could hear her. "Ah, but, Roque, my dear husband…would not it be more suitable if you were to make Bernadette a gift of the brooch? After all, I'm certain it would be more fitting worn at her throat…a scarlet brooch for a scarlet woman? Don't you agree?"

Bernadette drew in her breath in astonishment.

Roque was seething as Renee continued in a whisper, "Why don't we simply pin it to her bosom? And you, Roque…you could pin it there yourself."

He glared at her then, his jaw clenched with restrained fury. "You've spoiled my surprise, mouse. I shall have to think of something else to gift you for your birthday. Let us return home together, shall we?" he growled, taking her arm in his secure grip.

"Excuse us, ladies," Renee said, smiling at the group of old women as Roque led her from the mercantile.

Roque fairly dragged her along the street until they turned a corner and were out of sight of the astonished gossips. Taking her shoulders, he pushed her back against the outer brick wall of a building.

"What sort of scheme do you play at?" he growled.

"Me?" she exclaimed. "I've done nothing. Rather you have. You! You and your concubine unashamedly flirting in the mercantile!"

"What? I was attempting to procure a gift for you," Roque growled.

"Ah, yes! And Bernadette Sanders is just the woman to advise you on what would please me, is that it?"

Roque inhaled, clenched his jaw, and released her. "You're jealous," he stated.

Renee wiped the tears from her cheeks. "Jealous! Do not flatter yourself, Roque. Humiliated…naive, perhaps…but certainly not jealous." She began to quiver—overcome with emotion and the frigid breeze. "What a contemptible excuse, Roque. A birthday gift for your beloved wife? Couldn't you have attempted to conjure something more believable?" she sniffled.

"It is the truth. I thought you might like to receive a gift on such an occasion as your birthday," he explained.

"I don't expect a gift from you. You know that. It was a feeble excuse." She pulled on her mittens.

Unexpectedly, Roque chuckled. "A scarlet brooch for a scarlet woman. It was quick-witted on your part.

I'll give you that."

Renee looked up to him with yet tear-filled eyes. "Do not give me anything…not even recognition for owning wit. I don't want anything from you…ever!" she cried, moving past him.

Roque took hold of her arm, pulling her back to face him. "I tell you…it was innocent, Renee." She tried to struggle free, but he captured her, gathering her into his arms—holding her prisoner in his embrace. "And this I vow. You shall receive a thing from me as a gift for your birthday. Furthermore, I will give you a mere hint of its essence here and now."

Taking her chin firmly in hand, he kissed her—passionately kissed her.

Renee struggled, attempting to free herself from his arms and from his kiss—his kiss that she feared would overwhelm her own will in another instant. His mouth was hot and commanding hers, and she could feel her own soul willing her to surrender to him.

As her struggling began to diminish, his hand released her chin. Slowly—proficiently—he caressed her throat, causing her to tremble in his arms.

"Am I as distasteful to you as you pretend me to be?" he mumbled as his mouth left hers and pressed to the flesh of her neck just below her ear.

"Yes," she managed to lie in a whisper.

He chuckled. "You're a liar as well as a wit." He pushed at her chin, tipping her head back and forcing her to meet his gaze. "You shall have a scarlet brooch of your own to wear at the hollow of your throat. Rubies set into the shape of...hmm...perhaps the letter R, I think."

"For my name...Renee," she breathed.

"No," he said. His voice was low—alluring—wildly alluring. "Rather for mine...for Roque." He bent, kissing her persistently on the tender hollow of her throat. "And each time you wear it here..." Once more he kissed the place. "You will think of me...only of me." Again he kissed her there—allowed his lips to linger a moment before placing a moist kiss to her lips.

Though her heart was beating near to exhaustion—though she wanted nothing more in all the world than to know the warmth of his mouth to hers again—she pushed herself from his arms, saying, "I am not so easily distracted, Roque." Still breathless from the desire he had sparked in her, she cried, "You were consorting with her! You promised me your fidelity!"

"And I have, and will, keep that promise, Renee," he assured her. "I was truly only examining the jewels in hopes of finding a gift for you. Bernadette entered and began conversation. What am I to do? Ignore every person in town...freely offer offense for the sake that you are so easily provoked to jealousy?"

"Mrs. Montan! Oh, please! Only wait!" someone called.

Renee glanced over to see a woman approaching—Mrs. Shafer—who had once been her father's patient for many years. Renee remembered the woman was plagued by excessive pain in her joints and wondered what she was about on such a cold day.

"Mrs. Shafer? Whatever is the matter?" Renee asked as the woman reached them, gasping for breath.

"I heard you were near," the woman panted. Looking to Roque, she added, "Oh, sir, how glad I am that I have found you."

"Is there some trouble, madam?" Roque inquired.

"My daughter...you know her, Mrs. Montan...Sariah. Her baby is coming. The physician is not in, and I've no experience as midwife! Please, please come and help us! I know you have more

72

experience of this than I!" the woman pleaded.

"Of course we'll come. Only lead the way, Mrs. Shafer," Renee comforted, taking the woman's hand. "Come along, Roque. We may need your help," she instructed her suddenly mute companion.

Roque said nothing—gave no argument—but followed close beside her.

He did not speak until they had entered the small yet cozy home of Mrs. Shafer's daughter. "You have experience with these matters, Renee?" he asked in a whisper.

Though she was yet upset over what had transpired between her and Roque before Mrs. Shafer's appearance, she could not keep from smiling at him—for he owned an expression of bewildered astonishment.

"I am a physician's only daughter, Roque," she answered. "Who else do you think assisted him with bringing babies into the world?"

"She's in great pain, Mrs. Montan," a worried-looking young man said as Roque assisted Renee in removing her coat.

Instantly understanding the man was Sariah's husband, Renee gently said, "Of course she is, sir. It is a painful process. This is your first child?"

"Yes, miss…um, ma'am," the man stammered.

"Well, Mr.…"

"Charles Redman, ma'am," the man informed her.

"Well, Mr. Redman…this is Roque, my husband. He would be happy to keep you company during your wait," Renee said, motioning for Roque to come forward.

Charles took Roque's extended hand. "We're so glad you were still in town," he said.

Roque's only response was a rather uncertain grin and a slight nod.

Renee and Mrs. Shafer left the two men in the small parlor and hurried to Sariah. Renee frowned upon seeing the young woman, for she was obviously very near to delivering her baby.

"I'm Renee. Remember, Sariah? We went to school together," Renee said, squeezing the young woman's hand with reassurance.

"Yes," Sariah forced in response.

"You are near to having your baby out, I believe. Very well?"

Sariah Redman nodded, and Renee smoothed the perspiration from her brow.

74

Several hours later, Renee emerged from the bedroom with the healthy, pink baby girl wrapped snugly in a fresh blanket.

Roque and Charles stood as she walked toward them. "She is beautiful, Mr. Redman!" Renee exclaimed with sincerity. "Perfect and beautiful!" She offered the baby to her father, smiling at his awkward manner in cradling her.

"And Sariah?" Charles asked.

"She is very tired, but well," Renee reassured him, kissing the baby's tiny, fresh brow.

Renee looked to Roque, a smile of radiant bliss for the sake of the new baby still resplendent upon her face. "Do you see how beautiful she is?" she asked him.

Roque smiled in wonderment, staring at Renee. "Yes. I do," he muttered—yet not having looked at the baby.

"Look at her, Roque," Renee begged with delight. "She's perfect."

Roque did look then, and Renee could see the awe filling him as he smoothed the tiny head with one powerful yet tender hand.

"Congratulations, Mr. Redman. It seems you are truly a fortunate man," Roque said, placing a hand supportively on the other man's shoulder.

"How can we ever thank you, Mrs. Montan?" Charles asked.

"Only let me help with the next one," Renee chirped.

"Is she not a beauty?" Renee asked, bouncing along beside Roque as they walked home that evening.

The air was crisp and still, and the frost falling through the night sky reminded Renee of a dusting of diamonds.

"She is," Roque agreed. "I had no notion you were skilled as a midwife."

"Oh, yes. I helped Father quite often. I always found it a fascinating experience…witnessing the miracle of a baby being born."

"You're not miffed anymore then? About…earlier today?" he ventured.

Renee tilted her head back, letting the soft flakes of frost fall on her upturned face. "Yes. I am still angry. But for now, I'll let it pass," she sighed.

Roque smiled. "How kind."

The General was awaiting their return.

"How dare you, Roque!" he shouted as they entered the house.

"How dare I what?" Roque growled, instantly enraged.

Renee noted the manner in which Roque's mood—his very essence—altered upon his father's appearance.

"Letting her midwife to a common citizen of this town! It is unthinkable what diseases she may have been exposed to!" the General raged.

"I am well, sir," Renee assured him. "The Redmans are kind and good people, General. And I am grateful I was able to help them."

"You listen to me, girl," he growled, standing before her as if rage might set him ablaze at any moment. "You are in this house for one purpose! And well you know it by now! I have no use for you if you cannot serve said purpose. Therefore, take care not to cause yourself any blemish. Otherwise—"

"Otherwise nothing!" Roque shouted. "You will not speak to her again! Do you understand, General? Not one more word uttered from your lips, else I will take her from here."

Renee looked up at him in astonished dismay. Was he truly willing to leave the estate in order to protect her?

"There is no place I would not find her, boy," the General growled. "Idle threats do not concern me." Still, without another word, he turned and stormed away.

"Do not concern yourself with him, Renee," Roque grumbled. "He would not dare to touch you. He fears me more than you think he does." He removed his heavy coat and tossed it onto a nearby chair. Upon turning to face her, he sighed, saying, "I fear the new-fallen snow pales less than you." Gently taking her shoulders, he said, "I tell you…do not live in fear of him." He frowned, his eyes smoldering like firelit emeralds. "Have you so little faith in my ability to act as your protector?"

"N-no. No, I…" she stammered—for the sense of his touch had entirely scattered her thoughts.

"He would have need to kill me to reach you, Renee. Take comfort in that knowledge," he muttered, releasing her.

"Take comfort? Take comfort?" she exclaimed. "Take comfort in the knowledge that your very life is in danger? I would care not what happened to me if you were to perish! I would willingly sacrifice myself to your father before I would watch you…" She fell silent as he took her wrist.

"Contemplate such an atrocity…I will let him take my life there before you!" he growled. "That is the most asinine remark ever before uttered." Releasing her wrist, he inhaled a calming breath. "Now, rest assured, mouse…I shall not die at the General's hand…nor shall your virtue be compromised by, or for the sake of, the General's ambition."

"But why?" she asked.

A puzzled frown furrowed his brow. "What? Have I not made my intentions clear?"

"But why?" she asked once more. "Simply to best him? Is that the only reason you protect me from him? Merely to hold some advantage over him?" She paused, and when he offered no response, she continued, "If I were anyone, any other woman you happened to marry, you would swear the same oaths simply to best him. Would you not?"

Roque sighed with mingled defeat and frustration. "What is it that you want to hear, Renee? I cannot let him win. Put whatever diabolical reasons you wish behind it…yet I'll tell you this one last time. Then if you ask me again, I'll wring your lovely little neck myself." He reached for her, his strong hands gently encircling her neck. "He cannot win," he began, caressing her chin with his thumbs. "I have my own reasons...and perhaps one day you may understand them. For now, however, know that he is watching us...always watching us. Even at this very moment. I believe it boils his blood to see you with me," he whispered. "Thus, let us help the wound to fester, shall we?"

Yet Renee was not concerned over the General's spying in those moments. Roque's touch caused every other care to vanish! She watched as his eyes narrowed—saw the smolder of mischief and desire in them. He cupped her face in one hand, ever so slightly squeezing her cheeks, causing her lips to part. She gasped as Roque's mouth then applied an impassioned, titillating kiss to hers. His hand loosened its grasp on her chin—only held her face tenderly in place as his mouth continued to skillfully entice hers into responding with fervor.

She broke from him abruptly, covering his lips with her hand—for she feared she could not resist them.

"You are unduly cruel, Roque," she whispered.

"How so? Is he not cruel to you? To me?" he whispered, pushing her hand from his face in misunderstanding her.

"I was not speaking of your cruelty to your father…rather the callousness you issue toward me in trifling with me thus," she explained.

"You find my affections adequate then?" he chuckled.

"I find your abilities to seduce are masterful," she admitted. "I have no knowledge with which to judge your affections, however…for true affections are bestowed upon those to whom one holds a strong emotional attachment. Therefore, owning the knowledge that I do concerning my purpose in this house…I am not in a position to judge the merit of your affections…assuming, that is, that you even possess the capability of issuing them at all."

Renee forced her expression to that of indifference. She would reveal nothing of the great emotional and physical effect his kisses had generated.

"Well said, mouse," he grumbled as his own countenance hardened, "but naive all the same." He straightened—loosed the button at his collar. "You innocently delude yourself in many aspects concerning this circumstance. But no matter. For in two months' time you will be of age, mouse…thereby becoming the recipient of my masterful abilities to seduce…whether lacking of true affection or not."

"Do you make to threaten me?" she asked with defiance.

"Threaten?" he asked, smiling with mockery. "Rather a promise, mouse. A promise. Furthermore, whether or not you in conscious admit it to yourself, I have, only moments ago, been assured of your own inclination toward passion…exhibited, though I speculate somewhat reservedly, through your admirably restrained acceptance of, and participation in, the fevered kiss that I instigated previous."

Renee felt the hot blush rise to her cheeks—watched as he unfastened the remaining buttons of his shirt, stripping the garment from his body.

"Here," he said, wadding the article into a ball and forcibly pushing it into her arms. "Bury that pretty little reddened face of yours in this and familiarize yourself with the scent that is me…for you will come to crave that it be within your very breathing…just as you would thirst for water when lost in the barrens of a desert."

It was not necessary for her to inhale the scent of his clothing, for she knew it more truly than she knew the scent of summer roses—of the air around her—

of life. She knew that there was no aroma on earth that would ever bring her more joy—or pain.

"I am the vessel by which you are to beget your progeny, Roque!" she shouted, throwing the shirt at his head. "Not your laundress! And it does need washing...for it fairly reeks of a Montan!"

Dashing past him and up the stairs, Renee threw herself onto the bed she shared with her estranged husband—sobbing into her pillow.

Roque still had not retired to their bedchamber when she at last fell asleep. Some hours later, she awoke. There had been no sound to disturbed her, yet she woke to see Roque standing at the balcony doors of their bedchamber, gazing out into the night. He wore only his trousers, and his hands were clasped at his back.

"I am sorry that I was so condescending," Renee ventured—for she did not wish to own his loathing or to be the cause of further frustration to him.

He did not turn to look at her yet said, "I was wrong to speak to you in such a manner. He provokes the fiend within me." The fire in the hearth crackled, and Roque strode to it then, adding a log and stoking it with the poker. "Now that you and I

83

have, in essence, made our peace for the moment…you've known a very taxing day. Return to your sleep."

"And what of you? Are not you fatigued as well?" she asked.

"Indeed…but I prefer that you be sleeping before I retire," he muttered. "You…disturb me otherwise."

"Oh." Renee was discomfited, for she realized she must be a chaotic sleeper in order to disturb his sleep so. "I apologize. I will try to sleep as to be less disruptive to you." She was puzzled when he chuckled.

"Your sleeping habits have nothing whatsoever to do with disturbing me, mouse." He looked to her, the fire's flames reflecting in his mesmerizing eyes. "Your being a woman…you are not at the mercy of the same desires as am I."

"Oh!" she exclaimed as understanding penetrated her tired mind. She did, however, think his claim a bit naive—for the sight of him in his present state of undress sent her heart and senses whirling.

He chuckled again. "Now, to sleep with you, mouse," he said, raking his fingers through his tousled mane.

CHAPTER SIX

The morning of Renee's eighteenth birthday dawned, and she awoke to the knowledge that Roque's promise to her father was annulled at last—thus allowing the General's obsessive ambition to proceed. Gazing out the window into the bright winter morn, she pondered what it would feel like to carry Roque's child within her own body. She had always dreamt of having children—always hoped to have many. Each time she had helped her father bring a new baby into the world, it elated her—just as it had when Sariah Redman had given birth to her own gift from heaven two months previous. Even as the children in the township grew, Renee loved them. And to have her own, with Roque as their father, secretly she longed for it—for their children. Yet the General's presence clouded her joy, for he was demanding, dominating, and corrupt. She feared what a child living in his proximity would be subject to. Yet she had seen the expression of utter awe and wonderment vivid on Roque's face when he had first seen Sariah's baby. He would be a good, protective father. She knew he would protect them from the General.

"Happy birthday, my dear!" the General exclaimed as Renee entered the dining room where breakfast had been set. "And how are you feeling this morning?" he asked, smiling with triumph.

"No different than yesterday, sir," she answered. Roque was not present—and the fact unnerved her. "Where is Roque?" she inquired, for she had made a point of never being isolated with the General.

"Roque, you ask?" the General asked, feigning ignorance. "I believe the dear boy has run off into town. Some utter nonsense, no doubt. He makes himself such a busy man…wrecks himself on the rocks, you know. Won't you join me?" He gestured to a chair across the table from him.

"No, thank you," Renee declined. "I find I have utterly no appetite this morning."

"Now, now, Renee…we must keep your strength up. Especially after this greatly anticipated day, yes?"

"Most definitely, General," she answered, turning and casually leaving him to devour what remained of his meal.

As she exited the breakfast room, she bumped into Roque as he was entering it. Immediately her entire body began to perspire as the unsettling knowledge of what would ultimately transpire between them washed over her.

"Good morning, Renee," he greeted, raising an inquisitive eyebrow.

"A-and to you, Roque," she stammered. "Your father is already devouring his breakfast," she anxiously added.

"Thank you for the warning."

As she made to move past him, he barred her way by not moving from the doorway.

"Happy birthday," he whispered, slipping a small red velvet case into her hands. Then placing a finger under her chin, he tilted her face upward. "Guess what it is."

"No doubt a subtle reminder that I belong to you...completely as of this hour," she answered, feigning indifference.

"Well, not this hour," he amended. He removed his pocket watch, glancing at it. "Let me see...nine o'clock. Hhhmm. Fourteen hours more until you are officially of age." Again he tilted her face upward with a touch of his hand. "Are you reconciled?" he asked, his gaze searching hers for signs of resistance.

"Yes," she whispered as an abundance of moisture filled her eyes.

Roque caressed her cheek with the back of his hand. She did not miss the compassion in his expression.

"I will not force…"

Renee grew shy and glanced away. Yet she was touched in the same moment—for he had mistaken her tears as those of lost hope and fear when, truly, they were borne of delight in the knowledge she would at last be able to release him from the burden weighing him for so long.

He bent and kissed her tenderly on one cheek before turning and striding away. Renee watched him go—wondered what thoughts simmered within him.

"I have a gift for you as well," the General's voice boomed from behind her.

Renee turned to face him. "Really? Yet this is the only gift I wish to receive," she said, holding out the velvet box toward him as he came to stand before her.

The General took the case from her, opening it. His eyebrows arched with approval as he held the open case toward her. "Impressive," he said.

Renee's mouth fell agape with astonishment at what lay within the elegant case. As she had suspected, it was truly the initial R forged into the shape of a brooch. Yet the piece before her was no ordinary trinket the like of what she had seen at the mercantile. The piece before her was larger—elegantly crafted—gold set with many rubies.

"I interpret the initial to be R for Roque... correct?" the General asked as Renee took the case from him once again, marveling at what was within. "You will allow him his rights as your husband, now...won't you?" he more commanded than asked.

Renee looked up, loathing throbbing throughout her being. "Yes," she affirmed. "Do not pity your son any longer...for I know how you hold his best interests close to your heart, and his oath to my father is now null. He will be free to expect what he may from me."

"And you will—" he began.

"And I will cooperate," she spat, turning and marching from the room.

"My gift to you, Renee, is this," he called to her.

She paused before climbing the stairs. "I will leave this very afternoon...on business, you understand. I will not linger to provoke Roque to his violent mood this night."

How she hated him! As she slammed the door behind her, barricading herself within her chambers, she pondered on what an utterly loathsome creature the General was. How could one such as Roque be kin to him?

The hour was very late. Renee looked to the clock on the hearth as it struck eleven. The General had departed, true to his word, and Roque had been nowhere to be found since she had seen him that morning.

Perhaps he has changed his mind, she thought. Perhaps he still wished to vanquish his father at their horrid contest.

As the chamber door opened and Roque entered their room, she held perfectly still where she sat on the bed. Unexpectedly, an expression of defeat, unlike any Renee had seen him reveal before, washed over him. He sat down on the bed next to her, running his fingers through his hair in a gesture of having lost all strength.

When he looked to Renee, he appeared truly hopeless. "I swear to you, Renee…I thought this would be better for you," he muttered.

"What? Do you mean living here with wealth and social position, rather than orphaned and poverty-stricken?" Renee asked.

She sensed he had no intentions where she was concerned—that it had all been a ruse to irritate his father. She pulled the tattered red ribbon from her hair and began nervously twisting it around one finger. What had he in mind to tell her? She feared that he had come to rid himself of her somehow.

Again Roque let his fingers pull at his brown mane. He sighed. As he stood, stripping his shirt from his body, he said, "The General chose you."

"For you…I know," she said. "To bear your child and continue the Montan bloodline. I know it. How could I not?"

"No…or rather, yes," he mumbled, tossing the garment aside. "He chose you to assist in proceeding his own lineage, yes. However, he did not intend for you to do so by bearing my child."

Renee felt her very life's blood begin to chill as realization fully revealed his insinuation. "What are you telling me, Roque?" she asked.

He still did not turn to face her. "I am telling you what you are only now coming to realize. The General had seen you in town several months before your father became bedridden with his illness. He remarked on your unusual beauty and strength. He was angry with me for not having married, thereby producing the heir he so covets. He resolved that one son was not sufficient if the name of Montan were to remain eternally upon the earth. Thus, he decided he would marry again and produce other sons...on the chance that I would fail in my duties to the name I inherited."

Roque turned then, and the anger now apparent on his face troubled Renee. "He meant to marry you, Renee. He meant for you to bear his heir."

Renee clutched at her stomach, for it threatened to empty itself at the thought. "My father would not have agreed to it," she whispered.

"No. Indeed not. But the General would simply have waited until his death and then set about obtaining you all the same."

Renee looked up into the stern glare of her husband. "How then? How is it that you—"

Roque inhaled deeply—turned away once more. "I had seen you, of course. I remembered you as the little girl who burst into sobs at the loss of a hair ribbon. It did occur to me that you were nearing marriageable age. I have seen the General rain ruination on so many lives. I felt that I had to intercede in an attempt to halt his planning." He turned back to her. "I approached your father...explained that the time had come for me to marry and that I found you suitable. He was a desperate man, worried as he was about you...knowing that he would soon die. He agreed on one condition...and you know it. I thought the terms would be easy enough to maintain, for of course, I still viewed you as a child. But you've grown up, haven't you?"

"Yes," Renee spat. It was all too obvious. Roque had indeed intended to best his father, and in the process, he had broken her heart! She would not aid him any longer in his crusade against the General. "Yes, I have! And now I am old enough to serve your purposes well, am I not?" She slipped from the bed, sinking to her knees as sobbing wracked her. Yet her heartbreak bled to anger and took its aim at Roque.

She glared up at him. "You and your father are the most vile creatures on earth!" she cried. "How could you assume that I would merely serve as the

device with which to produce your children…
willingly and without objection? I am a human being,
Roque! Not a thing! Certainly not an animal! I deserve
respect, security…compassion. And what choice have
you left me now? I will tell you. Endure the abuses
and corruption of your father and bear his children,
which I will never be allowed to nurture and adore
thereafter…or submit to you, his son…and in
essence live the same life…a lonely, unhappy, loveless
existence in which I would dream longingly of death
as the only means of escape!" Renee buried her face
in her hands and wept bitter tears.

"I did not marry you for that purpose!" Roque
exclaimed. She felt his strong hands grip her
shoulders as he knelt before her. "Do you not see it?
I attempted to deliver you from just such a hopeless
existence as you truly would have known at his hand,
Renee."

Renee looked up into his beautiful emerald eyes.
"But," she began in a whisper, "you do not want me
at all."

Roque's jaw visibly clenched. She could see the
anger igniting within him once again.

"I am a human being as well," he growled. "You
have slept in my bed night after endless night…and I

have not moved to touch you. You are my legal wife. I have the right to expect…" He paused—stood— took hold of Renee's arm and pulled her to her feet. "You see the General in me, do you not?" he asked.

Renee shook her head. "No," she responded, realizing she had accused him in her heartbroken anger.

Though he frowned, Roque chuckled. "Yes, you do. You cannot look past the General to see me." Gathering her into his arms, he pulled her against him. "Very well," he continued. "If that is the way it is to be…then so be it!" His mouth seized upon hers—hot, moist, demanding. "The hour is upon us, mouse. My oath to your father bars me no longer."

"Please, Roque!" she cried, struggling in his arms. "Do not trifle with me!"

"Do not struggle so, Renee," he said. "I am certain the General would bestow no more mercy than I." She continued to struggle, however, and in Roque's efforts to restrain her, he tore her shirtwaist, exposing one graceful, pale shoulder.

Tightly he bound her in his arms as his mouth caressed her shoulder. Renee fought the sudden deluge of bliss erupting within her—but to no avail. She ceased her struggles when his mouth met her neck, ravaging her tender flesh.

"Stop, Roque," she whispered. She allowed one hand to caress his powerful, roughly shaven jaw and said, "I-I will...voluntarily submit to you."

Roque raised his head, gazing at her in disbelief.

Taking his handsome face between her small hands, she pulled his head toward hers, whispering, "I will submit to you... willingly."

As their lips met—began savoring intimate kisses—Renee's body began to weaken. Roque's arms held her firm as her knees faltered from the pure rapture evoked by his kisses.

He paused—broke the seal of their mouths. Taking her face in his hands, he searched her face for a moment, his eyes smoldering with emerald fire.

"Renee?" he breathed as his ravenous mouth again flamed a passionate indulgence between them.

She could perceive her heart was near to shattering for the sake of the love she had cached so deeply—and for so many months. Tears spilling from her eyes cascaded over her cheeks, trespassing upon the tempestuous kiss, and Roque drew away from her.

His eyes searched hers for a moment—misread her emotion as she looked away. Passion and desire lingered on his face—yet he growled, "I understand. I do."

Renee lovingly gazed back to him, but his eyes had grown cold and indifferent.

"The lesser of two evils, is that it?" he asked. "The least of the bitter roots to chew? It would be more conceivable…more tolerable…to endure my attentions than those of the General, would it not?"

Renee shook her head—brushed the tears from her face with the back of her hand. "No, Roque! Please…I…" she stammered.

"Well said, Renee! Well said," he mocked, clapping his hands in applauding her. "Yet fear not, my beauty. You'll not have to bear the burden of conceiving a Montan by way of me."

He turned to leave her but paused when she whispered, "But I want your baby."

Roque was silent for a moment. He glanced over his shoulder, saying, "You have to want me first, Renee." And he left her.

Oddly, Renee felt hope begin to well within her. For the first time since she had arrived at the Montan estate, she found true hope that Roque Montan could care for her in some regard—eventually. Oh, how she wished she had owned the courage to call him back to her—to tell him that she did want him—only him—that she loved him beyond his capability to imagine it. Yet in Roque's mind, he assumed she saw him as a younger image of the General. Perhaps he feared it was there himself.

Thus, Renee's eighteenth birthday passed—as did the weeks and weeks to follow—and without her receiving so much as a single desirable kiss from the man she so adored, loved—longed for.

CHAPTER SEVEN

Renee sensed the General's growing suspicion. He would repeatedly glance from Renee to Roque and back during their meals. He said nothing, yet she knew he would not remain silent much longer.

Renee had begun to wake in the early hours of morning, her mind spinning with anxiety and confusion. She wondered—if she were to confess all to Roque, her love for him, her passion for him, would it melt the hatred from his heart? Would he return a shred of her feelings? She would frequently lie in their bed watching him sleep—watching his massive chest rise and fall with the rhythmic breathing of unconsciousness. Often she would take a lock of his hair, curling it gently around her finger as she tried to find the courage to reveal her heart to him.

On one of these occasions, Renee smiled to herself as a vision entered her tortured thoughts—a vision of a small boy, her own dreamt-of child, the image of Roque, his dark hair tousled at first waking as his father's ever was. Habitually, she reached over, taking a lock of Roque's hair and curling it around her finger. She released it at once, however, when—without stirring or opening his eyes—he spoke.

"I have been enduring this every dawn for weeks, Renee," he mumbled. His eyes opened, and he glared at her, though his body remained still. "What is it that you ponder in the dark hours before the sun, while twining my hair about your finger?" he asked.

Renee turned away from him, stretching out on her back. She did not answer, for she was afraid her words would reveal too much. She did not meet his gaze when he raised himself on one elbow, taking a lock of her own hair and entwining it about his finger.

"This gesture…this toying with my hair," he began. "I know a certain woman—very literate in vocabulary—who might offer that this gesture." He brushed the lock of her hair against his lips. "Twisting my hair, as you do each morning…well, this scholarly woman, with whom I am very nearly intimately acquainted, might sort this particular familiarity as a display of…dare I utter the word…affection. Would she not?"

"I am sorry I disturbed you, Roque," Renee whispered, still not meeting his gaze.

"Do you shelter an affection for me, mouse?" he asked.

Renee reached over to the small table at her side of their bed, retrieving the scarlet ribbon that lay there. With feigned nonchalance, she pulled her hair back, tugging at the strand Roque held until he released it.

"I believe it is time to begin the day," she said, tying her hair at one side of her neck with the ribbon.

She began to sit up, but Roque's powerful arm stayed her—pinning her to the bed. He untied the ribbon, pulled it from her hair, and ceremoniously returned it to the nightstand.

"Tattered bit of adornment," he mumbled. "What sentimental reason could you have for keeping it ever near to you as you do?" He leaned over her, nuzzling her hair with his face—gently tugging at a strand of it with his teeth. "It is quite unsettling, is it not?" he asked, twisting a length of her hair around his finger once more.

"I do not do that," Renee said. A tiny thrill began

in her stomach as he again tugged her hair with his teeth—a tiny thrill that near instantly erupted into utter elation as he continued his flirtatious trifling.

"Not exactly…that is true," he admitted. "However, your breathing has quickened, mouse. Thus, I believe you understand my position."

His mouth descended then, pressing the hollow of her throat. He placed hot, moist, lingering kisses there, and when at last his kisses met hers, her trembling could not be concealed.

"Fear not, mouse," he mumbled, ending their kiss and caressing her lips with his thumb. "I only meant to have you wear my boots for a mile. No need to tumble into fearful convulsions." He turned away from her, pulling the winter quilt over his shoulders. "Now, run along and begin your day. I, for one, am still tired," he chuckled.

The incident that morning had disconcerted Renee. She had almost revealed her feelings to Roque—nearly confessed her love for him!

"What troubles you, my dear?"

Renee looked up to see the General looming above her. She had been alone in the bedchamber, but her anxious thoughts had occupied her, and she had not heard him enter.

"Nothing, General. Nothing in the world," she lied.

"Come now…I am family, after all. Let us have a moment of confidence. Does all go well between you and Roque?" he asked, lowering his voice to a whisper.

"Yes, of course!" she deceived once more.

"You seem unsettled…discontented. Roque has…well, he has…been attentive, has he not?"

Renee stood to face him, humiliation at his inference enraging her. "There is no need for you to question me on that matter! It is none of your concern!" she exclaimed.

The General's face reddened. "It most definitely is my concern, girl! Furthermore, your response has confirmed my suspicions!"

"You cannot force him to—" she began.

"No. I cannot…and I have been unceasingly patient with the two of you! Therefore, I see no other alternative but to take matters into my own hands." He reached out, taking hold of Renee's wrists then. "Come along, my beauty. The time has arrived for you to serve the purpose for which you were espoused!"

"Roque!" Renee screamed. Yet the General was not deterred. Savagely, he pulled her against him—so tightly bound her in his arms she could barely draw breath.

"Relax, my dear. It will—"

"Release her, or die where you stand, General!" Roque roared.

Renee looked up to see an infuriated Roque standing just within the chamber door.

"Roque! Help me!" she tried to scream—though she managed a mere whisper.

The General released her, and she ran to Roque, throwing herself into the safe haven of his arms.

"I will not allow her to linger under your roof any longer!" Roque shouted, enraged. "You are the most loathsome creature on this earth! Let the family name be hanged! I will not be the one to salvage it!"

Roque pushed her aside as the General pulled a pistol from beneath his coat.

"I am your father, boy!" he bellowed. "How dare you to threaten me!"

A bullet shot from the pistol, hitting Roque in the left shoulder. He stumbled, tripping over a nearby chair. Falling backward, his head met with the corner of a small table, and he was rendered stunned.

"Roque!" Renee screamed. She fell to her knees beside him, lifting his head onto her lap, stroking his hair. As her tears streamed from her eyes, she looked up to the General and cried, "You've wounded your own son! What kind of beast are you?"

"That you will know soon enough!" the General growled, taking hold of her arm and violently pulling her to her feet.

"You will have to kill me before you touch me," Renee sobbed, straightening with defiance.

"No. I won't," the General said. "What kind of a man is that?" he asked, pointing to where Roque lay still dazed on the floor. "No son of mine would marry a beauty the likes of you and not immediately bed her for the mere sake of some ridiculous agreement with her dead father!"

"Roque is honorable," she told him, her voice quivering with emotion. "He is not a merciless brute the likes of you! Furthermore, if you had not forced him into acting so rashly, perhaps he would have married someone he would have desired, loved, and wanted. Instead, your own repulsive intentions forced him into an act of unbridled chivalry, and he married me, rather than letting you debauch another soul."

"Well, my dear," the General chuckled, "in the

end, it matters little, for he has failed after all." He wound Renee's hair around one hand, yanking her head back.

Renee cried out in anguish as his sickening, foul mouth began consuming her neck.

"She is correct in her estimation of you," Roque said as he struggled to his feet. "You are vile and loathsome."

The General laughed. "Be a good boy, Roque, and close the door on your way out."

"I would pitilessly slay any man that would dare to lay a hand on her," Roque growled. "Your being the man who fathered me does not give you sanctuary."

Renee was gratefully aware of being ripped from the General's clutches and pushed to the floor. She looked up to see Roque's powerful fist meet with the General's jaw. The General reeled back but did not fall.

Roque moved, avoiding a blow from the General's fist. The General was doubled over, gasping for breath as a result of Roque's delivery of a second blow to his midsection.

"I am your father!" the General panted.

"No. You are an abominable human being whom

I have no wish to ever lay eyes upon again. Keep your name and the filth that you have caused to tarnish it. I will no longer have any part of it…save trying to nurture one honorable branch of my own."

"Take her from me, Roque…you will know poverty! You will be disinherited!" the General warned.

"I do not care. I never cared for or wanted your immense wealth. I never cared for you! Mother left me quite rich enough when she died. You did not know it, did you?" Roque asked. "That is because she did not want you to know. I had only hoped to restore some shred of honor to the name that she had endured with for so long…the name she died enduring. The very name I must bear. But it is not worth this. Nothing is."

Taking Renee's arm, he began to lead her toward the door.

"I will kill you, Roque," the General threatened, however.

Renee turned to look back at him—saw that he stood pointing the gun at his son once more.

"If you try to take her, I will kill you," he repeated.

Roque turned to face his father. "No, you won't.

Even you could not kill your only son, General." Then he turned and guided Renee with him as he left the room.

As they reached the top of the stairs, however, Roque pushed her clear of himself. She gasped as she saw the General charging toward Roque. Fury reddened the whites of his eyes, and he shouted as he lunged forward. Renee screamed as Roque adeptly moved to one side. The General was unable to stop the furious momentum that was powered by his rage. Renee watched in horrified disbelief as the General Maurice Montan tumbled top over bottom down the long case of stairs. The force of his body landing below echoed through the house with resounding finality.

Renee leapt to her feet, racing to the banister. With great trepidation, she looked down. The General lay unmoving but alive—his body apparently broken on the hard marble floor below.

"Renee!" he called in a pain-stricken voice. "Bring the physician for me. No doubt my son would leave me here to rot and be devoured by maggots."

Renee looked to Roque, who stood staring down—monumental hatred still seething in his eyes.

"I will bring the doctor, General," she said,

quickly descending the stairs. She paused, stood over the broken villain, and said, "For I believe you well know that Roque has been wounded."

❧

"I fear he may never walk again, Mr. Montan," the physician said to Roque as he changed the dressing at Roque's wound.

"It is no more than he deserves," Renee whispered.

"Imagine…shooting at his own son!" the physician mumbled. He looked to Renee, asking, "Are you well, Mrs. Montan?"

Renee nodded. "If Roque is to be well…then so will I," she whispered, watching as Roque's eyes closed. He slumbered at last.

"He will be well. He is a powerful man…and in good health. He will no doubt feel quite recovered by morning. The wound will be tender for some time…but Mr. Montan will be well."

Renee sighed with relief as the physician stood to take his leave.

"I knew your father, Mrs. Montan," he said. "He was a superior man and a profound physician."

"Thank you, Doctor Channing."

Renee saw the physician to the door and then

returned to sit beside Roque.

His eyes were closed, and he was breathing evenly.

She did not deny the impulse to reach out and smooth the perspiration from his forehead and was startled when he said, "That is, by far, the most ignorant thing I have heard escape your lips yet."

Renee retracted her hand from his brow. "What?" she asked.

Roque turned his head—opened his eyes—gazed at her. "Unbridled chivalry?" he whispered, grinning.

Renee was perplexed in not immediately recognizing her own words. Yet she smiled—cast her gaze aside as she did remember the words she had spoken to the General in regard to Roque's championing her.

"That red ribbon you cherish so," he began then, unable to keep his eyes open any longer, "is that perchance the same ribbon I once gave to you years ago…one day when your father was attending me?"

Renee still did not raise her gaze to look at him. "Yes," she answered.

He chuckled, and she did look up as he spoke. "Do you cherish it so because you value the ribbon…or because you care for the benefactor?" he asked.

Renee did not withhold the tears demanding release as she whispered, "It is most certainly the benefactor I cherish."

Roque exhaled a breathy laugh. "Then I have been a far greater fool than I thought myself to be," he said.

He uttered not one word more. Within moments, Renee was assured that he was indeed enjoying a deep, deeply deserved slumber at last. Gently, she lay down on the bed next to him. She knew his great fatigue would prevent him from waking easily again. Thus, she allowed herself the comfort of nestling against his strong, warm body.

Renee awoke to find the morning sun cheerily streaming through the window. She stretched—then realized Roque was no longer in the bed next to her.

"Roque?" she called as a great unease entered her mind. "Roque?"

Quickly she left the bed and hurried into the hallway. She smiled as she saw Roque making his way up the stairs with a tray laden with pastries in his hands.

"Calm yourself, Renee," he chuckled. "There are

certain things a man must attend to first thing in the morning…alone."

Renee sighed as relief at seeing he was well flooded her. Again a smile broke over her face as she observed his disheveled hair. It was apparent his strength was indeed returning.

As he reached her, his own smile broadened. "Whatever do you find so amusing each morning?" he asked.

"You. You are very…cute when you first awaken, Roque," she admitted.

"Cute?" he chuckled. "Puppies are cute, Renee. Not men."

She took the tray from him and smiled. "Cute is sometimes preferable, you understand," she informed him.

"As opposed to what?" he asked.

"As opposed to intimidatingly attractive," she answered. Embarrassed by her own sudden honesty, she turned and reentered the bedchamber, placing the tray on the table next to the bed.

Renee could feel that Roque stood directly behind her—his smoldering, emerald gaze searing the back of her head.

"I should tend to the General," she offered.

"Melba is with him. She will inform us if we are needed," he said.

"Well, then," she stammered nervously, "I suppose you would like to enjoy your breakfast."

She turned—moved past him and toward the door.

He caught hold of her arm, however, and her heart began to hammer as she turned to look up at him.

"I fully intend to devour it," he whispered, his eyes narrowing—fairly carving their way into her soul.

She resisted as he pulled her toward him, but he cocked his head to one side, daring her to challenge his advance. She did not, however—rather let herself be encompassed in his arms, her body drawn flush with his own. He kissed her forehead—nudged her head back, forcing her to look up at him.

"Do you care for me then, Renee?" he asked in a whisper.

She looked down and did not answer.

He tilted her face up again with one hand, and she gazed at him with plain longing.

"Do you love me, Renee? Do you want me…for your husband?" he asked.

"Are you asking me…reminding me that my age

no longer constitutes adherence to the agreement between you and my father?" she asked, her voice quivering with emotion.

"No," he answered. "I am asking you if you want me. For if you do not…I will grant you your freedom through an annulment."

Renee gasped as pain and fear tore through her heart. "Then…you do not want me at all? You want to be free of me?"

"Never!" he breathed. "You have no comprehension of how deeply I want you…crave you, in truth. Yet I do want you to be content. And if ridding yourself of an unwanted husband is the only way of contenting you, then I will…though most unwillingly…free you."

"You are trying to lead me into…you know that I…you want me to admit that I…" Renee stammered.

Roque chuckled. "Is it so hard to admit, Renee? To actually utter the words?" He cupped her face affectionately in his strong hands. "I love you, Renee. I'm asking…is it incomprehensible that you will someday return my feelings for you?"

Tears rivuletted down Renee's cheeks as she breathed, "You have known all along I love you…that I have ever been in love with you…since I was aged but twelve years!"

"I have not," he assured her as the smile faded from his handsome his face. "I truly thought you despised me…loathed the contemplation of my touching you. I will tell you further this. My resolve weakens daily. You are too appetizing for me to deny myself indulgence much longer."

Suddenly, Renee recognized the emerald smolder of his eyes: intense desire—restrained passion. She had mistaken this expression for anger and loathing so many times over the past months—when all the while…

"Then do not deny yourself," she ventured. Mindful of his wounded shoulder, she slipped her arms around his neck, pressing her body against his.

He did not hesitate—rather let his mouth know hers. His kisses were fiery—profound offerings of love—and Renee returned them with immeasurable fervor, allowing her love for Roque to guide her instincts.

Her mind was a whirlwind of wonder! Surely such a man as this could not possibly find in her all that he wanted—needed. Her own thoughts caused her to pull away—suddenly shy—disbelieving his sincerity in what was occurring between them.

Roque's breath was labored as he smiled at her with understanding. "I will prove it to you then…by means of my 'unbridled chivalry.' I will not attempt to seduce you—my own wife, remember—until such time as you believe all that I have confessed to you this moment." He chuckled at her perplexed expression, adding, "I will attend the General. Even he could not darken this moment for me."

He turned to leave but paused and looked back at her. "Desire demands that I ask—when next I attempt your seduction, how should I present myself? 'Intimidatingly attractive' or rather 'having just awakened cute'?"

Renee smiled. "You determine that for yourself."

He smiled at her and disappeared through the door. A moment later, he stepped back into the room, however.

"Oh, Renee," he began, grinning.

"What?" she smiled in return.

"Thank you," he said.

"Whatever for?" she giggled.

"For that immensely palatable breakfast you piqued my appetite with a moment ago." Chuckling, he disappeared from the doorway again.

❧

That evening, Melba informed Roque and Renee of the General's constant begging to speak with Renee. Nausea rose within her at the very thought of him.

"Please, Mr. Montan. I believe he is wishing to ask her forgiveness," Melba pleaded with Roque.

"No. I will go," Roque growled, rising from his chair.

Renee stood as well, trembling as she said, "Perhaps I should allow him to find his peace. He is weak, after all. A pitiful creature twisted now by the results of his wicked intentions."

Roque frowned. "You wish to forgive him?" he asked.

Renee shrugged. "What good can come of harboring hatred?"

Roque sighed and then nodded. "If it is what you wish…then I will linger close at hand should you need me."

"You may vex him," Renee said. "He cannot hurt me now. I will go alone to hear whatever he wishes to say to me."

Roque shook his head, but Renee placed a hand to his arm, and he nodded in relenting.

"Would you bring me some refreshment please, Melba?" he asked.

"Yes, sir," Melba said, smiling at Renee with grateful approval.

❧

Entering the General's chamber, Renee was startled at the sight before her. In the mere passage of hours, the once handsome, powerful man had become a bedridden invalid. The General motioned for Renee to move nearer to the bed in which he lay.

As she approached, he smiled at her—not the lustful, scheming smile she had come to know, but rather a sad and remorseful smile.

"Renee," he breathed. "Forgive me."

Renee frowned at him. "Forgive you?" she began. "You attempted to—"

"I know. I well know," he interrupted. "And I beg your forgiveness."

"Deathbed repentance is the phrase, I believe, sir," Renee stated.

"No. Simply repentance," he said. "I have seen my solicitors this day…while you and Roque were away from the estate. As of this very hour, everything I possess, save a small allowance on which I am to survive, is now given to Roque. I have lived a sinful, abominable life and deserve no better than to convalesce to whatever point possible, alone and in seclusion."

Renee was awestruck. His voice rang with sincerity.

He continued, "I would only ask that you somehow drive the hatred of me from Roque's good heart. Hatred can only destroy good, and I do not wish for his life to continue being dominated by it. Instead, let the love between you govern your lives. His mother was a marvelous woman…a rare woman. I brought her nothing but pain. I destroyed her, and I admit it now. He has her goodness…as will your children, no doubt. I will miss knowing them." He closed his eyes for a moment, weary, and Renee waited, for she sensed he was not yet finished.

"One last thing, daughter-in-law," he whispered weakly. "My son loves you. Do not doubt it. He would not have married you otherwise. 'Unbridled chivalry,' I believe you called it." He chuckled. "No, my dear…though Roque does possess that attribute as well, I have no doubt of it. I will tell you a secret now I never planned on revealing. It was Roque that brought you to my attention. 'How she has grown,' he said to me one day in town upon our passing you on the road. 'She will be near marriageable age now. I thought the day would never present itself to me!' he said. I am certain he had forgotten it was me at his side, for he surely would not have imagined that any other father would assume to acquire the young woman for his own selfish reasons."

"Do you mean to tell me—" Renee began.

"Yes, innocent saint that you are. Roque was only biding his time until you were at a reasonable age for him to court. I—villain that I am, my dear—forced him to play his hand abruptly. He will, no doubt, confess this to you at a later date. But I felt it necessary that it be confirmed by me as well."

As a flood of pure elation bathed her, Renee whispered, "I forgive you everything, General. I will melt the hatred and resentment from Roque's heart and…" She paused, contemplating the possibility of what she was about to promise. "And I will promise you that you will someday see grandchildren playing about the house…girls as well as boys."

A familiar, malicious laughter erupted from the invalid man's throat. Renee watched in horror as he tossed aside the quilt that had covered him. Deftly he rose from his bed to stand before her.

"Poor, gullible Renee," he growled. Reaching out,

he took hold of both her arms—painfully gripping them. "You are far too quick to forgive the sinner, Renee. Do you really think I would let you bear the offspring of that coward you call a husband?"

"Release me, at once!" Renee cried.

"Oh, quit struggling so, girl. It was inevitable from the beginning. I never intended for you to give birth to Roque's son! I only wanted another possibility of begetting a true Montan's son...a son untainted by a simpering, morally upstanding woman! You are young, strong, and beautiful. Thus, you will do."

"Roque! Help me!" Renee cried. Yet there came no answer—no beating or angry shouting from beyond the door—no salvation.

"Now, Renee. Lower your voice. What will the servants think?" the General whispered.

"Why? Why then did you have me married to your son?" she asked, trying to stall him. Her mind worked madly to think of a means of escaping the beast.

"For the simple sake of family name, my dear. Of course, everyone would assume that the child was Roque's. Therefore, the child would have a good name and future...all that he would need to succeed and carry on," came the reply.

"Do you harbor any sort of parental sentiment toward him? Have you no love for your own son?" she asked, shaking her head in disgust.

"He favors me in physical countenance…and I could perhaps love him for that alone. But there is too much of his sainted mother in him."

"It sickens me to think what misery she must have known in your presence," Renee wept.

"Now, do not worry your pretty little head, my dear. Yours shall be quite a different life, I assure you. For you are married to Roque…not to me." He dropped his voice and continued, "Now, reconcile yourself to the inevitable, Renee. It will go much easier for you."

Renee began to struggle fiercely again. "Roque will come! He will not allow you do this thing!" she screamed.

"Roque is most certainly asleep by now, my dear. Melba has already taken his soothing drink to him. He will sleep quite peacefully through the…proceedings."

Renee attempted to thrash about, kicking and clawing as the General's bitter mouth descended to her throat.

"Settle yourself, girl!" he roared. He held her arms at her back, causing great pain to her. Renee sobbed as she realized she was powerless and at his mercy.

As his mouth moved to her face, smearing repulsive kisses across her cheeks and brow, she cried out once more, "Please, Roque! Help me, please!"

As if in answer to her plea, the General stopped his assault abruptly as the door to his chamber crashed unobstructed to the floor.

There, standing furious in the lingering frame of it, was Roque. He was soaking wet from the waist up and swayed unsteadily.

"I warned you, Father," he growled.

"Roque!" the General mumbled, obviously astounded.

"I call you Father now…only for the sake that I think you should hear it once before your last breath is taken from you," Roque said. "Before I send you to rot in hell! For you will rot for sake of the abominations of your life."

"You'll not murder me, Roque," the General said, standing straight and confident once more. "For you are too good. It is against your very nature."

"Perhaps there is just enough of your blood in my veins to render me capable of it," Roque mumbled.

Renee watched as Roque entered the room—advanced upon his father.

"You will die…and you will die with the sure knowledge that she is mine! She will share my life, my possessions, and—so that your covetous, sinful mind can burn itself to a cinder—she will share my bed and bear my children! All this you will know through your eternity of perdition. And may it eat at your soul…if you have any soul about you."

"I intended that you should sleep through this, Roque…but I see you have somehow managed to thwart the calming potion I added to your drink. Therefore, it seems executing you is my only alternative action. How tragic that a young wife such as the lovely Renee should lose her husband of less than a year," the General sneered.

"Melba has always been more loyal to me than to you, General. She heard the danger for Renee and woke me, in the rather astonishing manner of emptying the contents of a bucket of water over my head. I have thanked her."

Melba appeared at the door then. Renee thought suddenly that Melba had always been quiet and reserved, but what shone on her face now was utter abhorrence.

"I watched you kill Roque's mother, Maurice," she spat. "I have turned my head and ignored your wicked, wicked deeds these many years…but I'll not let you cause the ruination of Roque's life."

"Why…you traitorous wench!" the General shouted. He lunged forward, hands outstretched and ready to grasp the woman's throat.

Just as he reached her, he cried out, and Renee watched in awe as he crumpled and fell to the floor—a knife embedded deep in his belly.

Renee looked up into the placid face of the maidservant.

"Melba!" Roque whispered in astonishment.

"The blood cannot be on your hands, young sir," she whispered. "You have too much life to live, and he has tainted it far too much already. He would have killed me, you know. I only defended myself."

Renee looked to Roque. His eyes narrowed, and he nodded. "I have no doubt of it," he said.

"I have got a daughter in a neighboring township, sir," Melba told him. "I would like this to serve as my resignation. No doubt the new lady of the house would prefer to employ her own servicing staff."

Not one more word passed over her lips. Melba simply turned and walked from the room.

Renee stood silent—still awed at what had just transpired. She looked to Roque—her beloved Roque—staring down over his expiring sire.

"I am truly sorry for you, General," he said as the man looked up at him. "But our lives are what we make of them, and you have done little good with your time on this earth."

The General clutched at the wound to his stomach. It bled profusely—draining the life from him. He looked to Roque mournfully—then to Renee.

"I sired the man beside you," he gasped. "Thus, I have offered one noble service to mankind...have I not?"

Renee nodded—forced a sympathetic expression. After all, he was a human being, and evil though he had been, he was correct. Roque was indeed an extraordinary gift to the world.

The man so near to death looked once again to his son. "I loved your mother, Roque. I want you to know that I did love her in the beginning."

Roque nodded in acknowledgement of the confession and said, "It is good to know...Father."

Maurice Montan exhaled his final mortal breath then. As his body grew limp and completely void of life, Renee looked to Roque. He stood unexpectedly sorrowful.

"It is good to know," he whispered.

❧

The constable and the physician had taken the General's body away. Roque and Renee Montan were left in complete and sweet seclusion.

"I believe he was sincerely penitent when the end came, Roque," Renee softly said.

"Seemingly so," Roque mumbled.

Renee could hear the all too apparent doubt in his voice.

"And I," Renee continued, "have vowed to drive the hatred of him from your heart."

"Difficult task," he said, exhaling a weary sigh.

"Perhaps," Renee agreed. Then, taking his hand, she led him down the corridor to their bedchamber. "Do you know…that your father confessed a grand and happy secret to me, Roque?" she asked as he sat down on the bed, grimaced, and pressed a hand to his wound.

"That being?" he asked.

"That being…that you had planned to marry me…even before he forced you to."

Roque quickly glanced at her—then away. "Oh. I

see. So now you think me a degenerate cradle robber because I have had my eye on you since before you were out of big long hair ribbons," he mused.

"No. I think now I can tell you without being so very fearful…that I love you, Roque. I always have, and if you have not known it…it can only be because you are truly an ignoramus."

He smiled. "Then I suppose I might interpret that as an encouraging remark." His mood was lightening. Renee sensed that, although he had just experienced an incident of tremendous emotional battle, he needed to be free of the effect of it for a time.

"Yes, you may," she giggled, moving to stand directly before of him. She ran her fingers through his immaculately brushed hair and whispered, "Now, I will share a secret with you."

Roque's arms slid around her waist, pulling her to him. He smiled at her—sending waves of anticipation and desire crashing over her.

"And what might that be?" he asked.

Inhaling a breath of courage, she began, "When you touch me…"

"Yes?" he prodded, handsome brow arched with curiosity.

"I feel as if I might literally burst into flames," she

confessed.

"Really?" he teased.

"Yes. And…and when you kiss me…"

"Mm-hmm?" he hummed as he kissed her throat.

"Well, in truth…I fancy that I might drop dead of a failure of the heart muscle," she whispered, mesmerized as he moistened his lips.

"Is that so?" he whispered.

"Yes," she admitted with brazen truthfulness.

"And," he began, reaching up to rake one hand through his hair in order to tousle it. "And how do you find me now, Renee?" he asked.

"Irresistible," she sighed.

She possessed now a certainty that they were liberated. The evil threat that had churned their lives for so long—kept them from one another—had expired. However pitiful its end, it had indeed ended. Freedom was theirs—freedom to love, to live a life wholly their own.

Roque kissed her then, and as his mouth worked to possess hers, her own willing mouth met his.

"Do you play at seducing me, wife?" he asked, his breath warm on her lips.

"No, sir. I am quite seriously intent upon it," she answered, gazing lovingly into the emerald fire of his eyes.

"Finally," Roque breathed as he kissed her. "Finally."

AUTHOR'S NOTE

The General's Ambition marked the debut of several very important firsts in my writing career: the first time I used the title of the book as a catch phrase in the story—the first time I was daring enough to use the word "lust" (scandalous, I know!)—and perhaps most importantly, The General's Ambition is the first book wherein the hero strips off his shirt! But let's talk more about "firsts" later, shall we?

Let's begin with Kristy Jo, for when I first penned The General's Ambition, it was as another gift for her. Now you must understand that Kristy Jo has the vocabulary of a Victorian poet! It's one of the things I admire and adore about her—the incredible command she owns of the language. She's like a walking dictionary! And let me tell you this: the woman can spell! Seriously—like without spell-check and stuff! She and I used to play a little game whenever we were isolated together in the car or just sitting around at her house; we would spell to each other rather than merely speaking our conversation. By spelling to each other I mean we would literally spell out every word we were saying. In truth, the game never lasted long—because Kristy Jo could spell paragraph after paragraph without pausing to draw breath, while I was good for about six or seven sentences before my mind would mush out.

Yep, Kristy Jo liked words—and this is the reason you may have found a few words in The General's Ambition that made you go, Huh? Words like acrimonious, concupiscence, and vaunting. You and I may have to visit dictionary.com to learn how to use them in a sentence, but the Victorian poets wouldn't—and neither would Kristy Jo! Furthermore, rare or unusual words intrigue me! I like to play "Thesaurus" in my head sometimes—think of as many synonyms for a word as I can, just for fun. And you know how I love poetry, especially poetry written long, long ago—you know, the real sappy stuff, written when people expressed their sentiments for nature and one another though the artful stringing together of words. I marvel at how a poet or an author can take a few words and create a vision, a feeling—evoke emotion and profound thought. Thus, there are several "word of the day" words in The General's Ambition originally planted in the text for one purpose: to entertain me and Kristy Jo. I did later discover, however, that all my friends enjoyed a good Huh? word now and then—even if the reason was simply that they knew I liked weird words!

And now onto a little ditty I like to call "The Roque Issue." Believe it or not, when I first started writing, I usually just slapped a name on most of my characters—didn't really think them out before I started like I do now. I'd have a character's personality in mind back then but just wanted to get the story out before it flittered away. So most of the time, I'd just whack any old name down, thinking I could go back and change it later. However, The General's Ambition was the first time I really thought about the hero's name for a while before I christened him with it. I can't remember where I heard or saw the name Roque—or if I simply dreamed it up because it looked like the word rogue and I liked that word. Anyway, I liked the name and decided to name Roque, Roque (pronounced rowk). However, in true "Marcia" style, I had to go and way overthink it. I figured his name couldn't be simply Roque; it seemed too simple. So I agonized awhile and decided his full name would be Roqueford—only everyone would refer to him as Roque.

So I went along my merry way and wrote The General's Ambition—wherein Roque was the first hero to strip off his shirt and dazzle the heroine with his "massive chest"—and all my friends adored it! Thus, la-dee-da I went along after having written this book—for literally ten years. And then it was suggested that I allow my "early work" to be made available to readers via an e-book format. That's when "The Roque Issue" hit the proverbial fan!

When the "early books to e-books" plan was presented, I had already changed some of the character names in my earlier books. As I said, most of them had run around the world with names I had simply plugged in and never gone back to fix. However, Roque's name was the one name I liked, and I planned to leave it just as it was. But good ol' doubt never stays silent long, and when a newly acquired friend said, "Roqueford? Roqueford? It sounds like a stinky cheese!"—well, I panicked! A stinky cheese? How romantic is a wheel of stinky cheese, no matter how good he looks with his shirt off? Yep—panic—that was my reaction. I was already a nervous wreck about allowing readers to read the books I cut my teeth on, and now I was afraid they too would think of a wheel of stinky cheese when they read Roque's name! Ahhhhhhhhh!

Well, obviously Kevin wasn't around that day to calm me down; thus, a contest commenced. Readers were asked to submit their suggestions for new hero and heroine names for The General's Ambition. Though I was impressed, pleased, and delighted over the number of submissions, as well as the number of good suggestions, I was somewhat disenchanted. I went ahead and chose winners from the contest submissions—and "Roque and Renee" became "Merrick and Madalynne." There was a little preface-type thing included at the beginning of the e-book version of The General's Ambition, explaining that I was nervous about allowing the public to read it. I stated that I hadn't been satisfied with the hero and heroine names, explained about the contest, and said that I was concerned basically because the General is such a lewd character. Then I let it go—in theory. What I realized shortly thereafter is that I was fine with the names of the characters—especially if I just dropped the '-ford' from Roque's name so that the reader envisioned a rogue and not a wheel of stinky cheese! Roque and Renee were Roque and Renee! Peer pressure and doubt had trumped my staying true to myself, and I had caved. It's one reason I'm so grateful this anthology is being made available; it gave me a chance to apologize to Roque and Renee—to stay true to myself! And besides—I like cheese!

Oh, that reminds me—the whole "hero strips off his shirt" thing—it's a tale to tell! When I first began letting anyone other than Kristy Jo read my stories, I was worried about the whole "Roque strips off his shirt and tells Renee to become familiar with the way he smells" thing. However, let's just say this: all my friends loved it! I think everyone vacillated between being intrigued, astonished, delighted, amused, and the urge to whistle and applaud. I didn't really plan to have every hero thereafter stumble across the need to rip his shirt off once or twice in every book; it just came naturally. I mean, let's face it—that's what heroes do, right? So, again, I went merrily la-dee-da along—writing books for my friends—heroes and heroines having adventures, falling in love, and kissing—and not even consciously realizing that each hero (starting with Roque Montan) always found a way to pull his shirt off in the heroine's presence.

(I must pause here to share a little ditty. A big, buff, menacing Marine once walked up to me and said, "I'm not gonna let my wife read your books anymore." Entirely intimidated, I still somehow managed to ask, "Why?" He simply answered, "Because last night she told me that I take my shirt off wrong!")

So, anyway, as I was saying, la-dee-da I went along—merrily along for years—writing away and making copies of my books for friends. Well, then I was published, and the year my first book was published, a group of my dearest friends and I (a.k.a. the Groovy Chicks) were having a little Groovy Chicks Retreat. Being the good friends that the Groovy Chicks are, they were excited about my books being published. However, in the course of a conversation during that little Groovy Chick getaway, one of them suggested that I might forget about them while writing—that I might not write my books with them in mind anymore. I promised them that I could never do that, and we all began to think of a way that I could assure them of it. But how? How could I let all of my closest friends know that I was always thinking of them—always remembering the crazy, silly fun we used to have sitting around reading my books together—when we all lived so far apart and my books were going to be available to the world? And then—epiphany! It was suggested that in every book I ever wrote, the hero had to find a way to strip off his shirt. That way, those dearest friends—who not only had always been supportive and encouraging but also had loved my books along with me—would know I was thinking of them! Oh! Ryder Maddox took off his shirt! Marcia's thinking of me! they would think. Oh, look! The Crimson Knight is in his pavilion without his shirt off again! Marcia's thinking of me! Thus, just as the term "massive chest" (which made its debut in The Unobtainable One) became a catchphrase among my friends, my heroes stripping off their shirts became a tried-and-true Marcia Lynn McClure tradition.

(Trivia Note: Other than The Unobtainable One, there is one story I've written wherein I literally forgot to have the hero remove his shirt. Do you know which story it is? If so, fear not—for I do plan on rectifying that profound mistake sometime in the future!)

Thus, you know a little history of The General's Ambition—not to mention being further assured that I'm pretty goofy sometimes. Hmm, let's see—goofy, daffy, nutty, dippy, dotty, kooky, whacky, silly, and—finally—sappy. (That ol' thesaurus in my head never sleeps!)

~Marcia Lynn McClure

The General's Ambition Trivia Snippets

Snippet #1—In writing The General's Ambition (as I was winding up to the end), I had originally planned to have Roque kill the General when he finds him "man-handling" Renee. However, I had never had a hero kill anyone before, so I chickened out. (It was only my second story, after all.) So instead, I had the General fall down the stairs and get hurt—thought I'd end it there. But then I started thinking, Hey! Maybe he should have the chance to do the deathbed repentance thing. Thus, the birth of the scene where Renee goes into his room and the General is all remorseful and stuff. But no! I thought next. He was a jerk! A lewd, evil, lustful villain! It was obvious he needed to be out of Roque and Renee's life forever. Yet I was still too chicken to have a hero kill a villain (even though that is what heroes do—just like taking off their shirts). So in the end, Melba killed him. (In rereading it in preparation for its release with this anthology, I kept thinking, It's like all those action movies where you think the villain is dead and then all of a sudden he pops up out of nowhere and gets killed again, and then he pops up out of nowhere and gets killed again. I'm an idiot sometimes.)

Snippet #2—Because of part of the plotline (you know—the General's ambition to assure the continuance of his name and bloodline no matter what), my friends and I always referred to The General's Ambition as "The Lewd Book." And you had to string it out like this when you said it—"the looowwdd book."

Snippet #3—Okay, so you know the whole thing where Renee has been fiddling with Roque's hair when she thinks he's asleep, so he takes a strand of her hair and starts playing with it, and then she tries to pull it back with the ribbon, and he takes the ribbon away and starts playing with her hair again, and then he brushes it against his lips and tugs on it with his teeth? You know that part? Well, real-life inspiration hits again!

There was this guy—I didn't have a crush on him

or anything. He was a drummer, a real suave and cool guy, and we got along really well. We went out a couple of times, but I never really had any thought of actually "dating" him. Do you know what I mean? However, there was one thing this guy used to do to me that I thought was way, way, way…well, I guess titillating would be the word. Whenever we were dancing, he'd fiddle with my hair—with his mouth! Seriously! It might sound kind of weird, but it was awesome! We'd just be dancing—you know, back and forth, back and forth, the whole sway thing—and I'd feel him brush his chin against my hair. Gradually, he'd begin to brush his lips against my hair—you know, just real lightly—and then I'd feel a little pull as he tugged at it with his teeth. Seriously—I loved it! I mean, the whole thing was so fascinating and provocative that I can't even tell you! I didn't even like that guy in any romantic regard, but I was all like, Holy Guacamole! And that, my friends, proves just how good that little method of flirtation was!

To my husband, Kevin…
"Perfectly Imperfect" to Perfection!
A Perfect Dream Come True!
Forever My Perfect Hero!

About the Author

Marcia Lynn McClure's intoxicating succession of novels, novellas, and e-books—including The Visions of Ransom Lake, A Crimson Frost, Shackles of Honor, and The Whispered Kiss—has established her as one of the most favored and engaging authors of true romance. Her unprecedented forte in weaving captivating stories of western, medieval, regency, and contemporary amour void of brusque intimacy has earned her the title "The Queen of Kissing."

Marcia, who was born in Albuquerque, New Mexico, has spent her life intrigued with people, history, love, and romance. A wife, mother, grandmother, family historian, poet, and author, Marcia Lynn McClure spins her tales of splendor for the sake of offering respite through the beauty, mirth, and delight of a worthwhile and wonderful story.

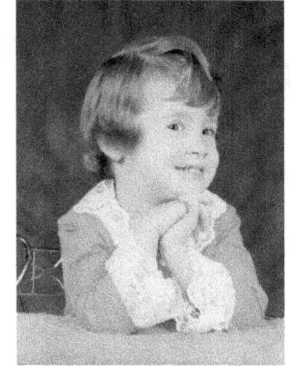

BIBLIOGRAPHY

A Bargained-For Bride
Beneath the Honeysuckle Vine
A Better Reason to Fall in Love
The Bewitching of Amoretta Ipswich
Born for Thorton's Sake
The Chimney Sweep Charm
A Cowboy for Christmas
A Crimson Frost
Daydreams
Desert Fire
Divine Deception
Dusty Britches
The Fragrance of her Name
A Good-Lookin' Man
The General's Ambition
The Haunting of Autumn Lake
The Heavenly Surrender
The Highwayman of Tanglewood
The Horseman
Indebted Deliverance
Kiss in the Dark
Kissing Cousins
The Light of the Lovers' Moon

Love Me
The Man of Her Dreams
The McCall Trilogy
Midnight Masquerade
The Object of His Affection
An Old-Fashioned Romance
One Classic Latin Lover, Please
The Pirate Ruse
The Prairie Prince
The Rogue Knight
Romance at the Christmas Tree Lot
Romance in Sleepy Hollow
The Romancing of Evangeline Ipswich
Romance with a Side of Green Chile
Saphyre Snow
Shackles of Honor
The Secret Bliss of Calliope Ipswich
The Stone-Cold Heart of Valentine Briscoe
Sudden Storms
Sweet Cherry Ray
Take a Walk with Me
The Tide of the Mermaid Tears
The Time of Aspen Falls
To Echo the Past
The Touch of Sage

www.ingramcontent.com/pod-product-compliance
Lightning Source LLC
Chambersburg PA
CBHW071525170626
46811CB00007B/2950